NO LONGER PROPERTY OF
ANYTHINK LIBRARIES/
RANGEVIEW LIBRARY DISTRICT

D0056831

THE LAST MIRROR ON THE LEFT

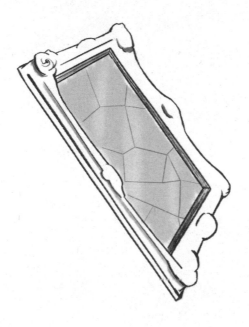

THE LAST MIRROR ON THE LEFT

By
LAMAR GILES

Illustrations by *DAPO ADEOLA*

VERSIFY
Houghton Mifflin Harcourt
Boston   New York

Copyright © 2020 by Lamar Giles
Illustrations copyright © 2020 by Dapo Adeola

All rights reserved. For information about permission to reproduce selections
from this book, write to trade.permissions@hmhco.com or to Permissions,
Houghton Mifflin Harcourt Publishing Company, 3 Park Avenue, 19th Floor,
New York, New York 10016.

Versify® is an imprint of Houghton Mifflin Harcourt Publishing Company. Versify
is a registered trademark of Houghton Mifflin Harcourt Publishing Company.

hmhbooks.com

The text was set in Adobe Caslon Pro.
Title hand lettered by Maeve Norton
Designed by Whitney Leader-Picone

Library of Congress Cataloging-in-Publication Data
Names: Giles, L. R. (Lamar R.), author. | Adeola, Dapo, illustrator.
Title: Last mirror on the left / by Lamar Giles ; illustrated by Dapo
Adeola.
Description: Boston ; New York : Versify, Houghton Mifflin Harcourt, [2021]
| Audience: Ages 10 to 12. | Audience: Grades 4–6. | Summary: Otto and
Sheed, The Legendary Alston Boys of Logan County, are ordered by Missus
Nedraw to bring a fugitive to justice in a world that mirrors their own
but has its own rules.
Identifiers: LCCN 2019036656 (print) | LCCN 2019036657 (ebook) | ISBN
9780358129417 (hardcover) | ISBN 9780358130437 (ebook)
Subjects: CYAC: Adventure and adventurers—Fiction. | Time—Fiction. |
Supernatural—Fiction. | Cousins—Fiction. | African Americans—Fiction.
| Science fiction.
Classification: LCC PZ7.G39235 Law 2021 (print) | LCC PZ7.G39235 (ebook)
| DDC [Fic]—dc23
LC record available at https://lccn.loc.gov/2019036656
LC ebook record available at https://lccn.loc.gov/2019036657

Manufactured in the United States of America
DOC 10 9 8 7 6 5 4 3 2 1

4500806348

For Aaliyah, Jaiden, Laurence, and your future cousins

kangaroo court

(noun) a court held by a group of people in order to
find someone guilty of a crime or misdemeanor
without good evidence

1

Sheed's Probably Going to Punch Otto

IN THE OPINION OF SHEED ALSTON—one half of the duo known as the Legendary Alston Boys of Logan County—his cousin Otto (the other, more annoying half) sometimes needed to be punched.

Sheed had come to the conclusion a few years ago, when Otto got on this whole dinosaur thing. Don't get it twisted —dinosaurs were, and still are, super cool! But even something super cool, like dinosaurs, became less cool when Otto insisted on knowing every single fact in the world about them, then insisted Sheed know that he knew every single fact in the world about them. All day. Every day.

Like, okay, Otto, a lot of movies got it wrong, because some dinosaurs had feathers . . . but did he ever think movies don't show that because then the dinosaurs would look like chickens and that's just dumb?

Around the fourth time Otto mentioned that the

heaviest dinosaur was the Argentinosaurus and it weighed ninety tons, Sheed had had enough. He'd slugged Otto in the chest.

Not a hard punch. He didn't want to *hurt* Otto. It was just enough to make a point. Otto stopped talking about dinosaurs so much after that.

And now that Otto was onto a new topic, one so much less cool than dinosaurs, Sheed knew another punch was coming. For sure.

"Did you know," Otto said, "doctors who play video games are twenty-seven percent faster than doctors who don't?"

It was Saturday in Logan County, Virginia. The sun was shining. The leaves were shifting from green to brown/orange/gold, and they hadn't had any legend-worthy cases lately so Sheed wanted to eat his Frosty Loops with just the right amount of milk—the loops only damp, not soggy—in peace. Then maybe ride bikes to Fry Park and do flips off the swings. He did not want to talk about doctors. Again.

"Faster at what?" Grandma sang. She had choir rehearsal that afternoon, and while she worked the dough for the biscuits she was taking to the church, she also practiced. Low notes, high notes. Their conversation was at least one half song. Sheed didn't like this tune, though.

"Diagnosing illnesses," Otto said. "And surgeries. They make fewer mistakes, too. Do you think Dr. Bell plays video games?"

Grandma cut off a high C note and resorted to her speaking voice, giving her vocal cords a break. "I don't know about that. Dr. Bell likes fly fishing, I heard him speak on that many occasions."

"People can like fly fishing and video games, Grandma. Maybe you should make an appointment for me and Sheed, and we can ask him."

Sheed dropped his spoon into his Frosty Loops bowl, splashing milk on the table. He leaned into Otto and whispered through clenched teeth, "Are you crazy?"

Visiting Dr. Bell usually meant *shots*. That man was scarier than the dentist and were-bears combined.

"We're overdue for checkups," Otto said, looking at the floor. "They're important."

"Stop. Talking." Sheed flexed his punching hand.

Grandma left her biscuit dough alone and checked the teacup-pig calendar on the wall, humming while she flipped back a few months. "Y'all went at the beginning of summer. We barely into fall, so you don't need a checkup yet." She crossed the kitchen, rubbing dusty flour on her apron before pressing the back of her hand to Otto's forehead. "You feeling all right, sugar?"

Sheed wondered the same thing.

"I'm fine, Grandma." Otto still wouldn't meet Sheed's eyes.

"What about you?" Grandma said, reaching for Sheed.

Sheed tried to execute Maneuver #1 (run), but Otto

turned full traitor and grabbed his wrist so he couldn't get away. He was so getting punched when they were alone.

"Hold still," Grandma said sharply, and Sheed knew better than to resist.

When she pressed her hand to his forehead, she said, "Hmm."

Grandma then grazed his cheek. "You do seem a bit warm."

"I'm fine, Grandma. It's just hot in here from the oven." He slipped away, headed upstairs, cranky because he knew his Frosty Loops were too soggy now—the optimal milk absorption window was a narrow one—and he was almost certain his cousin had just bought him a trip to Dr. Bell's. What was wrong with Otto?

"Rasheed Alston! I know you ain't stomping up no stairs in my house!"

Sheed stopped stomping. "No, Grandma."

Otto padded out of the kitchen but skidded to a halt at the base of the stairs when Sheed gave him the *we have unfinished business* look they saw all the time in kung fu movies. Otto said, "Um? Where you going?"

This! On top of doctors-doctors all the time, Otto acted like he couldn't let Sheed out of his sight for one second these days.

"To brush my teeth!" Sheed said. At the top of the stairs, he entered the bathroom and slammed the door.

"Rasheed Alston! I know you ain't slamming no doors in my house!"

"No, Grandma."

He sat on the edge of the bathtub, cupping his chin in both hands. If there was a way to mess up a Saturday, leave it to Otto to discover it.

A couple of sharp knocks sounded. Sheed yelled at the door, "Leave me alone."

Two more knocks, like he hadn't said a word. Not from the door, and not even close to the sound you get when knuckles hit wood. This sound was a hollow echo. Maybe a pipe? The house was old so that happened sometimes. He leaned into the bathtub, ear angled toward the drain.

Two more knocks, followed by a voice that almost made Sheed run screaming.

It said, "I know you're there, Mr. Alston. I'd prefer not to be rude about this, but you and your cousin have already worn my patience razor thin."

Sheed stood slowly, tracing the sound to a place it should not be coming from: the mirror over the sink.

When he faced it, the usual sight — his own reflection — was not where it should be. Instead, the mirror had become something like a window, looking into an all-too-familiar building. The Rorrim Mirror Emporium in downtown Fry.

Obscuring the view of the massive mirror warehouse was the magically weird proprietor of the emporium.

"Missus Nedraw?" Sheed said.

"Of course it's me. I require you and the annoying one's assistance. Get him now. Chop-chop!"

Sheed had no idea what this was, but he and Missus Nedraw agreed on Otto being annoying, so that was something.

2
Upon Further Reflection

GRANDMA GOT BACK TO HER BISCUITS, and Otto returned to the kitchen table, sulking, to finish his Frosty Loops. He wasn't hungry anyway. His appetite had taken a real beating in the last few weeks.

It was Saturday in Logan County, Virginia. Clouds kept blotting out the sun—and Otto usually liked clouds. The leaves were drooping and dying. It was starting to get chilly, which meant everybody at school would be sniffly with extra snot. Otto missed how things were before the last day of summer, when everything had gone so terribly wrong.

Since that day, there'd been so much on his mind, so many observations and not nearly enough deductions. All about his cousin. None more important—and terrifying— than the one that changed everything.

If Otto didn't do something, Sheed was going to die.

Maybe not next week, or even next year, but there was no timeline that Otto would accept. Hadn't he himself come from the future—as the traveler TimeStar—to keep from losing Sheed? Didn't he have to do everything in his power to complete the mission TimeStar had given him?

He shoved his Frosty Loops aside and left Grandma to her singing and baking. He drifted into the living room and flopped in his favorite spot on the old lumpy couch, where he fished his notepad from his pocket. Otto did his best thinking on paper.

OTTO'S LEGENDARY LOG, VOLUME 24

ENTRY #25

Sheed's not going to ever WANT to go to the doctor, and I can feel him getting super annoyed with me. It's the dinosaurs all over again. BUT, if it saves his life, I'll be annoying.

DEDUCTION: Keep working Grandma. If she believes Sheed is sick, she'll MAKE him go to the doctor, and we can maybe get a jump on whatever's wrong with him.

Of course, it had occurred to Otto that he might simply tell Grandma what he knew. Or tell Sheed. Every time he felt he might break and spill it all, he was reminded that he — *TimeStar*—hadn't conquered the laws of time and space, hadn't come back to Logan County from decades in the future, to run to Grandma. TimeStar also hadn't revealed his true identity to Sheed. It was a secret Otto was meant to keep. And fix. On his own.

To save Grandma the pain he'd felt when he deduced there was no future for Sheed. To save Sheed the knowledge of death chasing him with much less distance to make up than anyone would've expected. To—

"Otto! Come up here, please."

Uh-oh. Sheed said please. I'm definitely getting punched now, Otto thought.

But it would be worth it if Otto saved him.

"Why do you want me to come up there?" Otto wasn't necessarily eager to catch hands.

"I can't find the toothpaste. I need your help."

Nope. Not falling for that. "It's where it always is."

"The *special* toothpaste. Now, get up here!"

The special—? Oh, this was one of the new maneuvers. #83: Put *special* in front of something that's *not* special, so you know something actually special—*Logan County Special*—is happening.

Grandma was too busy kneading her dough and

humming her church songs to catch on, so Otto slipped away, stuffing his notepad into a pocket on his cargo pants while creeping upstairs very carefully, in case the Logan County Special thing had Sheed hostage or something.

At the top landing, Sheed's head protruded from the bathroom, his Afro pick wedged tight in his hair, and he waved Otto over. If this was a punching trick, it was a good one, because Sheed didn't look annoyed at all. He looked scared.

"What is it?" Otto asked.

Sheed grabbed his shirt, yanked him inside, then shut the door behind them. "Look."

He pointed at the mirror that wasn't doing what a mirror was supposed to. It looked more like a TV screen, and Otto did not like the footage being displayed.

Otto said, "Missus Nedraw?"

She cleared her throat. "Yes, I'm right here."

"Ack!" Otto shouted.

"Ack," Missus Nedraw said, drolly, "is correct. There's more 'ack' than I care for going on today, and you two are going to help me fix all the 'ack.'"

Otto said. "What's wrong?"

Missus Nedraw sneered. "Of course you have no clue. You think you can do whatever you want and your choices won't affect those around you. It's the same sort of short-sighted inconsiderate behavior that lands my prisoners where they are. You two should be glad we're addressing this early. With my intervention, perhaps I can turn you . . . you . . . *criminals* from your wayward path before it's too late."

The boys had only recently discovered the truth about the Rorrim Mirror Emporium. That it was a prison. The various mirrors it housed were cells, the prisoners locked behind the glass. Missus Nedraw was the warden.

Otto and Sheed accepted what should've been an over-whelming discovery because it was made on that strange last day of summer, and honestly, there were weirder things happening. Now the idea of a secret mirror prison hidden in downtown Fry, and the truly insulting comment Missus Nedraw just made, required some revisiting.

"Don't call us criminals!" Sheed said. "Grandma told us not to let anyone call us out of our names. We haven't done anything wrong."

"In fact"—Otto kept his voice low because he didn't want Grandma hearing, though he was about to make a good point that deserved to be heard—"we're the premier heroes of this county. The opposite of criminals. Legends. Thank you very much."

Missus Nedraw nodded sharply and paced on her side of her the mirror, with her arms clasped behind her back, giving them a full view of the crowded emporium floor as she left the mirror frame, then returned, blocking their view until she disappeared on the opposite side.

She didn't look like her normal, put-together self. Usually

she wore wool jackets over frilly blouses with high collars, long skirts, and striped socks with boots. Her mouth was always pinched, her glasses spot-free, and her silver-black hair pulled into a flawless tight bun. From what Otto could see of her, the outfit was about the same, just messier. The jacket seemed smudged with crusty stains. One lens of her glasses was cracked. Stray hairs protruded from her scalp at odd angles, like she'd had an unfortunate run-in with some aggressive static electricity.

Otto grabbed his notebook while she wasn't paying attention, scribbled furiously.

ENTRY #26

Missus Nedraw looks like a hot mess.

DEDUCTION: Something's happened at the emporium. Something bad.

She retraced her steps a few times, appeared to be thinking mightily. Then she stopped in the dead center of the bathroom mirror frame and said, "So you'd like the court to believe that you are not criminals?"

"We're not," Otto and Sheed said at once.

Then Otto thought, *What court?*

Missus Nedraw said, "Tell me, then, who took mirrors

from my emporium, without permission, to fight a being named Mr. Flux several weeks ago?"

The boys said nothing.

"Need I remind you," she said, "that you are under oath?"

Sheed said, "No, we're not. What?"

Sheed looked to Otto, perplexed. Otto shook his head. He didn't know what she was talking about either.

Missus Nedraw wobbled a bit, like she was dizzy, or weak. It didn't stop her crazy talk. "Well? Who took mirrors from the emporium?"

Reluctantly, Otto raised his hand.

"What's it called when you take something that does not belong to you, without permission?" she prodded.

Otto couldn't bring himself to say it. Mostly because he knew she wasn't wrong.

"Stealing," she finished. "You two stole from me. That is a crime."

Otto didn't like lies. Almost as much as he didn't like secrets. But he needed to clear up one thing. "Sheed didn't have anything to do with it."

Which was true, because Sheed had been Mr. Flux's captive when Otto orchestrated his plan.

Sheed, however, jumped in. "He did it to save all of Logan from being frozen forever. How do you even remember?"

That was a good question. They'd changed the past, and

to the best of Otto's knowledge, no one should remember the true events of the last day of summer outside of him, Sheed, TimeStar, and Petey Thunkle. Yet . . .

Missus Nedraw said, "The emporium and I are a part of the Multiverse Justice System. A constant throughout time and space, boys. Temporal reality may bend, but the law does not!"

Sheed said, "What the heck does that even mean?"

"It means your little stunt had consequences. Grave ones. That you need to help me rectify. We've wasted enough time. Come to me before I come to you. You have one hour."

Missus Nedraw slapped a palm flat against her side of the glass, and the mirror became a mirror again, displaying the boys' terrified faces.

Sheed said, "What does she want?"

"I don't know," Otto said, twisting the doorknob, "but she said one hour. I don't think we want to be late."

3
Smoke and . . . You Know

IT TOOK APPROXIMATELY FIFTY-NINE MINUTES and thirty-two seconds for Otto and Sheed to reach the emporium.

First, they had to convince Grandma they were just going to play. Then convince Grandma that even though the weather man said it might be chilly today, they'd be okay without coats. But they didn't actually convince Grandma of that one, so they had to dig their coats out of the box marked WINTER THANGS, then convince Grandma they'd be warm enough with *just* coats—not gloves, scarves, and knit hats. Finally, she was convinced that scarves would be enough, and that left them nine minutes to bike into town with itchy wool coiled around their necks, trailing them like kite tails.

Otto was actually grateful for the short time. Riding their bikes that hard and fast didn't leave any breath for Sheed to complain, though Otto did tail him the whole way to make sure he wasn't using *too much* breath. Worrying about Sheed had become his new pastime, as habitual as jotting notes in his log or chasing Keys to the City. As necessary as school and Grandma's food.

On Saturdays there were a lot of city folk making day trips into the county, mostly headed into town for the farmer's market. As the boys came upon the WELCOME TO FRY, VIRGINIA sign, they passed Mr. Percy Ellison's truck at a stoplight, filled with bushels of the corn he sold at the Ellison's CORNucopia table. Wedged in among those bushels were Wiki and Leen—the Epic Ellisons—eyeing the boys warily.

Wiki, suspicious, yelled, "Where are you two going in such a hurry?"

Lingering too long around Wiki gave her opportunities to find the most obscure clues to any secrets you might be trying to keep, so Otto scooted past her fast. "Errands for Grandma!"

"I saw your liar tic, Octavius Alston."

Otto swung a left, uninterested in a mental tug of war with Wiki that day. And when he swung that left, he shot right past Sheed, who'd slowed to make googly eyes at Leen.

"Hey, Leen!" Sheed said, waving while steering his bike one-handed.

"Hey, Sheed!" she replied, leaning so far over the truck bed Otto worried she might fall out.

Those two.

"Watch it!" someone yelled.

Otto hadn't been looking where he was going. An angry, snarling beast reared up on its haunches a dozen feet ahead of him. He squeezed his hand brake and swung his back tire forward, canting his entire bike before planting one foot to bring him to a stop inches from the creature's snarl.

Its lips peeled back, revealing long, slick canines. The muscles in its haunches coiled like springs, preparing to pounce, its jaws ready to maybe eat Otto's face. A second before it launched itself, a white-coated streak bounded from the sidewalk and slipped a muzzle over its snout in one smooth motion.

Dr. Medina, Fry's veterinarian said, "Now, now, Walter. Don't go scaring the poor boy."

It was way too late for Walter not to do that.

Walter, whatever he was, seemed confused by his sudden inability to devour Otto if he so chose and thrashed against the muzzle. In that moment of confusion, Dr. Medina clamped a leash onto the spiked collar Otto had only just noticed. She dragged Walter back to the open door of her animal hospital. The reluctant animal gouged deep furrows into the asphalt with claws Otto was happy to observe at a distance.

Sheed coasted to a stop next to Otto and said, "What is that, Dr. Medina?"

Through clenched teeth, the muscles in her neck straining, her eyes squinted from exertion behind the bright red frames of her glasses as she fought Walter's leash, Dr. Medina said, "A wolverine."

Both boys were pretty certain wolverines weren't native to the city of Fry, or Logan County proper. Though they were on the clock, Otto felt the need to jot down a single note in his pad.

Look into Dr. Medina. Soon.

They were back at it, legs pumping steady, just two minutes before Missus Nedraw's deadline expired and who-knows-what happened. They turned onto Main Street, shot past Archie's Hardware, the Big Apple Bakery, the Lopsided Furniture Company, and the other staples of Fry's business sector, and leapt off their bikes at the entrance to the Rorrim Mirror Emporium. When they crashed through the doors of the warehouse-like building, its shelves and shelves of hand mirrors, makeup mirrors, full-length mirrors, wall-size mirrors, disco-ball-like mirrors, and so on yawned before them. They sprinted down the aisles, their lungs screaming for air. It felt like they'd run a mile, way too far for the size of the building—or at least how it appeared from the outside. Finally, in what Otto figured was the center of the emporium, they found Missus Nedraw perched on a stool, an old-timey stopwatch *tick-tick-tick*ing in her palm.

Only when the boys skidded to a stop before her, crouched, their hands planted on their knees while they sucked air, did she jab the stopwatch's button, silencing it. "Twenty-eight seconds to spare."

"How," Sheed panted, "is this place so big?"

"Magic, boys. As you may know, ninety-nine percent of magic is smoke and what? Say it with me."

"Mirrors," Otto and Sheed managed to wheeze out together.

Sheed spoke between gasps: "What kind of . . . magic . . . did you use . . . to talk to us in our bathroom? I don't . . . want you to use . . . that magic again."

"The BMMCS is less magic than marvel, child."

"BMMCS?" Otto said.

"Bathroom Mirror Mass Communication System. Most advanced way of connecting people in the universe." The next part she said singsongy, like a jingle: *"All it requires is a name and desire."*

Sheed said, "Like when Grandma tells Siri to call Miss Eloise from church?"

"It's way better than Siri. But yes, I suppose."

"If it's so good," Otto said, "why doesn't everyone use it?"

"Well," Missus Nedraw said through a sneer, "it seems many people aren't so eager to have conversations with others from their bathrooms."

Sheed said, "I kind of figured."

"Enough about that." Missus Nedraw gave a stiff nod. "You met my deadline. No need for any harsh punishments. Yet."

"Punishment?" Otto said, "What kind of punishment?"

"That would've been up to the Judge. Thankfully, we don't need to bother him over any tardiness."

"What Judge?" Sheed asked.

"Let's hope you never find out. For all of our sakes."

Sheed wouldn't let it go. "That's not good enough, Missus Nedraw. You should tell us what this is all about! Calling us down here all spooky-like."

Uh-oh. Sheed was revving up. Normally, Otto would shrug off a Sheed tantrum, but what if him getting angry somehow made his body weaker? Made his sickness come faster?

Otto's hand drifted to his cousin's back, rubbing soothing circles the way Grandma might if one of them was in bed with a bad cold. "It's all right, sugar."

Sheed's eyes bugged. He slowly sidestepped until he was out of Otto's reach. "Don't ever call me that again."

That was *too much* like Grandma, then. Noted.

Sheed, clearly uncomfortable, focused all his attention on Missus Nedraw, who still hadn't told them what this was all about. Otto noticed a conspicuous green wall behind the emporium's proprietor.

The wall was tall, running well into the gloomy shadows of the ceiling. There were patches where the paint was lighter than the rest of the wall. Those patches had distinct shapes. Some oval. Some rectangular. Some Otto wasn't sure what to call . . . just fancy. He glanced around at other walls; none of them were bare. Mirrors were hung on them, floor to ceiling, in neat rows. He whipped out his notepad.

ENTRY #27

There used to be mirrors on this wall, too. They'd been mounted there for so long, the wall darkened around them. The shapes are where their frames had pressed against the original paint.

DEDUCTION: Someone took those mirrors down, and it wasn't Missus Nedraw. Not if she's this mad.

"Look!" Missus Nedraw pointed to the highest and lightest patch on the wall, where a single ornate frame once hung. "See what you've done?"

Sheed said, "Um, no."

"Then let's take a closer look, shall we?" She walked to a nearby counter and jabbed a red button mounted next to an old-fashioned cash register. In the rafters above, gears began to grind.

A rickety, shuddering platform of some sort dropped slowly on cables. Otto's first thought was *elevator,* but it didn't come all the way to the floor, instead stopping level with where the highest missing mirror had been.

"Come on." Missus Nedraw motioned to a series of plain, full-length mirrors aligned along the base of the opposite wall. She scooted between the boys and moved briskly toward one of the mirrors. The boys followed, confused. Missus Nedraw did not slow as she drew near the glass of one mirror. The boys flinched, anticipating a collision, like when birds fly into a clear glass door. They still hadn't gotten used to the way things were here.

Missus Nedraw walked directly through the glass, meeting no more resistance than if she'd walked through fog.

Above them, on the platform, was another full-length mirror that Otto hadn't noticed. Missus Nedraw materialized from the glass of that mirror as easily as someone steps through an open door.

"Teleportation," Otto whispered. Amazed. He jotted down his observation.

Missus Nedraw crossed the shaky catwalk and pointed at the space the missing mirror once occupied. "See? Here?" She looked over her shoulder, seemed flummoxed by the boys not being behind her on the platform, then leaned over the safety rail, radiating annoyance. "Are you coming?"

Sheed frowned. "Naw. Just tell us from there."

She huffed. "Fine. The mirror that used to be here housed the most dangerous prisoner in the emporium. He broke out. Thanks to you. If you don't help me retrieve him, I'm going to lock you in a mirror for . . . well, forever."

4

This Is Not the Way to Motivate People

"UMMMM," OTTO SAID. "WHATCHU TALKING ABOUT, Missus Nedraw?"

Missus Nedraw waggled her long finger at him. "You helped facilitate the escape of one of my most dangerous prisoners. You're an accomplice."

"I am not!"

Missus Nedraw reversed course, stomping back through the mirror on the platform and instantly emerging from the mirror on the ground level with the boys.

"When you took mirrors without my permission," she said, "you and your friends were careless. In your haste, someone managed to bump Nevan's frame, cracking his mirror. The crack was small enough that I didn't notice it, but he sure did. He worked at it little by little—like one of you normal human prisoners digging a tunnel with a spoon. Now he's loose and he's taken his gang, the Despicable Dozen, with him."

Otto moved closer to the empty wall. Tiny glass shards crunched under his sneakers. Remnants of a destroyed mirror. "When?" he said.

"Last night. I was settling in for my evening tea when I heard a crash. I ran out here to see what all the commotion was about. I glanced up, saw Nevan's mirror was gone, and . . . well . . . I take it he bonked me over the head, because the next thing I remember, it was morning and this entire wall was bare."

The more aggravated she got, the more wispy strands of her gray hair worked loose from her bun, making her look wild and unhinged. "Because you meddled with the emporium when I explicitly told you not to, any destruction Nevan brings about will be on you, and the punishment is imprisonment. Though given your stature in the community, I'd be willing to ask for leniency on your behalf. Perhaps I could get you one of our roomier mirrors."

Otto was stunned.

Sheed said, "You're not putting him anywhere. He didn't do anything wrong. The town would still be time-froze if it wasn't for—"

An urgent ringing interrupted Sheed. Like a telephone, but it seemed to sound from every corner of the emporium. And not just sound; the bright white fluorescent bulbs over their heads flashed red in rhythm with the shrill tone, tinting everything crimson.

Missus Nedraw seemed to shrink right in front of the boys. Her arms fell slack at her sides. The scowl she'd been directing at Otto flattened. Her neck craned up at the same moment a long gold-and-silver-framed mirror lowered from the ceiling.

"Boys, hide. Right now," she said. No-nonsense.

"But—" Sheed began.

"Right. Now." Missus Nedraw was stern again, the type of stern Grandma was when there was a really bad storm and she made them all sit in the big downstairs closet where there were no windows until the worst passed. The scared kind of stern.

So, Maneuver #2. Hide. They bolted and hopped the counter, crouching beneath the emporium cash register. Neither could resist peeking over the countertop as the long fancy mirror stopped inches short of bumping the warehouse floor. The ringing and red lights continued.

Missus Nedraw attempted, in vain, to flatten her stray hairs—they popped right back up. She tried smoothing the wrinkles in her clothing, wincing at her own reflection. The ringing and flashing were more persistent, so she placed her palm flat on the glass and said, "Answer."

This must've been one of the communication mirrors, just bigger than the one in their bathroom, Otto reasoned.

Missus Nedraw's reflection dissolved in a swirl. The boys gasped at what—or who—replaced it.

It—he? (the boys weren't sure)—hunched to fit the frame, even though the mirror was taller than Missus Nedraw by a foot. The being on the other side of the glass had long, oily black hair that fell over his face, covering his eyes, a pale blue-gray nose and cleft chin protruding between the strands. He wore a black robe. Tucked under his left arm was a massive leather book, the pages rough and yellowed. In his right hand was a tall staff made of rich oiled wood and topped with a cylindrical head—a double-sided mallet of sorts. Flat on both sides, meant to pound. It did not have the rough, deadly look of a weapon, though. As strange as the staff was, Otto couldn't shake the feeling that he'd seen something like it before.

The being spoke. "Warden, report."

That voice was like an echo from a grave. Deep enough to vibrate your bones. Sheed grabbed Otto's sleeve, as if to make sure he wasn't alone with anything that sounded like that.

Missus Nedraw, for her part, sounded calm. "All is well."

A message contrary to what she'd told the boys moments before.

"Well?" The being leaned closer to his side of the glass, and the mirror bulged outward. "The fugitives have been apprehended?"

"They are safe in a mirror."

He returned to his original posture, nodding. "This pleases me. I can't tell you how disappointed I was to hear of how irresponsible you'd been." He motioned to the book under his arm. "I was reviewing the Law for an appropriate punishment."

Missus Nedraw's chin thunked on her chest. "I understand, sir. What was your verdict?"

He chuckled, a sound like a fist slowly knocking on a coffin. "This time . . . mercy."

Missus Nedraw sank to her knees. "Oh thank you, Judge. Thank you so much."

Otto and Sheed locked eyes. *That's the Judge?*

Then Otto knew where he'd seen that staff-mallet-thing before. In all of Grandma's judge shows—*Judge Jamila, Judge Jorgé, Judge Jessi-Anne Jenkins*—they closed cases by banging a "gavel" on their desks. This judge held the biggest gavel ever. Maybe because sentencing someone to eternity in a mirror was such a big deal?

"Mercy this time," the Judge said. "If there ever is a next time, I may not be so lenient." He held that thick leather book for her to see. "The Law is the law."

Missus Nedraw gathered herself to her feet. "I understand, Judge."

"Excellent. I will be by soon to inspect Nevan's new cell."

"H-how," Missus Nedraw stuttered, "soon?"

"Does it matter? All is well. Is it not?"

"Yes, yes. Of course. Drop by anytime. Anytime at all."

"I plan to." The Judge raised his gavel, struck the base of the handle sharply on the floor. The mirror winked to a normal reflective surface again; cables reeled it to the ceiling. A shaken Missus Nedraw craned her neck, watching it go.

Otto and Sheed emerged from their hiding place. While Otto scribbled in his pad, Sheed went on the offensive. "You told us this Nevan guy escaped. But you told the Judge that he was safe in mirror."

Missus Nedraw said, "I did."

"So you either lied to us or him."

"No. Both things are true. Though 'safe' was an exaggeration." Now she sounded as nervous as when she'd spoken to the Judge. "Nevan escaped with his evil gang. Into another mirror."

Otto glanced up from his notes. "How can he escape if he went into one of your cells?"

She waved a hand, indicating they should follow, talking while she led them past intimidating tall shelves that made up an unknown number of aisles. "Not all mirrors are cells, meant to hold things. Some, like the one in your grandma's bathroom or the one the Judge used, are for communication." She motioned down an aisle crammed with a variety of bathroom mirrors, perhaps thousands of them.

"Some are short-range passages, like the one I used to get on that high platform earlier." She waved a dismissive hand down another aisle crammed with tall mirrors in plain frames. More of the teleportation mirrors, Otto presumed.

"And some"—she rounded a corner and came to an abrupt stop before an aisle that ran between two seemingly infinite rows of tall, colorfully framed mirrors—"can take you much further."

Missus Nedraw let that sink in. Otto jotted it down.

ENTRY #28

Some mirrors = prison cells.

Other mirrors, like in Grandma's
bathroom = windows that you can talk
through (though most people don't like to
have conversations in the bathroom).

Some are teleporters for relatively
short distances.

Then . . . there are the mirrors that
are something else entirely.

DEDUCTION: I don't like where this is
going . . .

"Nevan went down this aisle and through the last mirror on the left. Perhaps the most dangerous of them all."
Missus Nedraw shuddered. "And we're going after him."

5

A Warped Perspective

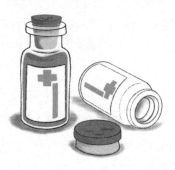

THERE WERE, LIKE, A MILLION MIRRORS stretching as far as — farther than — the eye could see.

Okay, maybe not a million. But a lot. For sure.

An odd, seeping gray mist slithered between them into the aisle. If this was one of those smoke and mirror tricks, Sheed thought it was a darn good one.

Missus Nedraw led them deeper down the aisle. With every mirror they passed, the glass showed different things that were a mix of reflection and something more.

On their left, one mirror's frame was coral colored, overlapping pink and beige. Its surface wavered like water; Otto's and Sheed's reflections swished. Sheed could've sworn he heard the ocean.

On their right, another mirror's frame was made from blood-red wood. At the top corners were carved claws, set to look like some vicious monster skulked behind the mirror, attempting to climb over and attack. The glass was tinted dark, and Otto didn't like his reflection in that one at all. He looked ashy, almost see-through, like his reflection wasn't all there. When he sneered at the ghostly version of himself, he thought he saw fangs protruding from his mouth.

They continued down the very long aisle and came upon a mirror that was covered by a silky black veil. Sheed felt drawn to it like a magnet. He stopped before the veil. "What's up with this one?"

A few steps ahead, Missus Nedraw and Otto paused. She said, "That's a Black Mirror. It stays covered because the reflections can be upsetting."

"Like how?" Sheed pressed.

"When you look in that one, you see what you look like on the last full day of your life."

Otto immediately grabbed Sheed's sleeve and dragged him along mumbling, "Nope, nope, nope."

"I wasn't gonna," Sheed whined, unsure if he totally believed himself. It *was* a little tempting.

After what felt like an hour, they came to the end of the aisle. The mirror Missus Nedraw finally stopped at had a frame carved from the cheap wood of bargain dollhouses and discount coffee tables. It was painted in bright primary colors, and at the top was the image of a jolly clown. An abandoned wagon sat before the mirror, similar to the one they'd seen her load up with mirrors (a.k.a. prisoners) and take for a walk along Fry's Main Street.

"This was how Nevan moved the mirrors that held the members of his gang," Otto said. An easy deduction.

Sheed frowned at the glass. "What's wrong with this mirror?" He shuffled slightly to his left, tilting his head and squinting. "Did Nevan break it?"

"No," said Missus Nedraw. "It is functioning as intended. I suspect that's why Nevan chose it."

Sheed's reflection was not accurate. At all. He appeared to be several inches shorter and wider, the glass showing something akin to a mushroom with legs. When Otto stepped before it, he got the opposite effect. He appeared taller and stick-figure slim. Thin enough to wriggle through a keyhole. Missus Nedraw stepped behind them, and her head ballooned to a shape that shifted from wide to flat as her chin tilted from one boy to the other.

"It's like a funhouse mirror," Otto said, rotating his body so the image warped to something else unexpected.

"Exactly," Missus Nedraw said. "And not. Most funhouse mirrors don't allow for interdimensional travel to another world."

"Interdimensional travel?" Otto said.

"Another world?" said Sheed.

Their other questions came in a quick, barely audible rush.

"Is it an opposite world?"

33

"Is right really left, and is up really down?"

"Do people have their hearts on the other side of their chests?"

"Would a compass point south instead of north?"

Missus Nedraw raised her hands, flustered. "Boys, boys! Listen. It's none of those things. A mirror world isn't the opposite of the world you come from. Its properties, and people, and rules are . . . *reflected* . . . by the mirror itself. The way this glass warps what we see"—she pointed, and her tiny fist and index finger became the size of a watermelon in her reflection—"is the way the world beyond exists. Some things will feel the same." She rotated her hand in a way that made it appear normal, if only for a second. "Most

things will seem illogical. Unpredictable. Unexpected. It's a frightening place."

Sheed considered this, picking nervously at his 'fro. "A Warped World."

"Yes. A world of chaos. The differences between that world and the one we're in may be small, or large. They will definitely all be strange."

Otto wrote, not looking up. "You think Nevan chose this mirror for a reason. Why?"

"Because, despite the best efforts of the Judge and all who follow the Law, the world on that side of the mirror remains defiant and unruly. Things can change on a whim, and anyone who goes there may suffer the effects for better or worse. Nevan is a small and angry monster with delusions of grandeur. If he spends enough time in such a twisted place, there's no telling what he may become."

"Godzilla?" Sheed said.

Missus Nedraw pursed her lips. "No. I don't think he'd become Godzilla."

"But you don't know for sure." Sheed waggled a finger, feeling victorious in making that point.

Missus Nedraw sighed. "It might be as bad as Godzilla. All right? Can we stop dragging our feet now and go get him?"

Horrific possibilities that had nothing to do with Nevan or Godzilla flitted through Otto's head. "I don't know, Missus Nedraw."

She said, "You must come with me to undo what you've done."

"I didn't do any—"

Sheed cut Otto off by grabbing his collar and dragging him a few steps away for a private conversation. "Otto, this is kind of the sort of thing that we do."

Otto shook Sheed off. "Yes! Yes it is!"

"So what's the problem?"

Part of the problem was this ridiculous accusation on Missus Nedraw's part, how she kept saying this was somehow Otto's fault. Part of it—the bigger part—was Otto hadn't planned on taking any more cases, going on any more adventures, or doing anything else otherwise legendary until he found out what was going to make Sheed sick and how to fix it. But he couldn't really explain that, could he?

Sheed said, "It's because this probably won't get us a Key to the City, right? I hate to be the one to tell you this, but you get really selfish over those things."

Otto flinched. This wasn't about him at all! Angry and bitter, he said, "Yep, that's me. Selfish Otto."

"We should help Missus Nedraw."

"Right." Otto stomped past Sheed, bumping his shoulder on the way. "What do you need us to do?"

Missus Nedraw said, "Simple. You can be my navigators."

Sheed said, "Huh? You said the world is warped there. How can we navigate through a strange place we've never been?"

"Warped. Not new. When we go through the mirror, we'll be in a version of Fry, which will exist in a version of Logan County. The things we see, and the people we meet, may seem odd. At the core, though, there will be some familiarity for those who know this place the way you boys do."

Otto said, "You live in Fry, too. Why isn't it familiar to you?"

"Sadly, I don't get out of the emporium much. I'm not as immersed in the community as you and your neighbors."

Something felt wrong about Missus Nedraw running a secret prison in a town where she couldn't be bothered to get to know her neighbors. Grandma always said a community should be like extended family. Knowing each other and counting on one another. This might not be the time for a Grandma lesson, though.

Missus Nedraw said, "Are you ready?"

"Now?" both boys said at once, standing before their wobbling reflections in the warped mirror.

"Now."

"Do we need any supplies?" Otto asked, flipping to a blank page, ready to make a list.

"Maybe some weapons?" Sheed offered.

Missus Nedraw placed a hand on each of their shoulders. "We'll discuss."

She shoved them face first into the Warped World.

6

Welcome to My Parlor

THE BOYS FLINCHED as their wacky warbling reflections —and more importantly, a pane of glass—rushed toward them. They expected smooshed faces, busted lips, maybe even broken shards of mirror that scraped and cut. As was often the case in Logan County, the natural gave way to the *super*natural. Instead of a collision, there was the momentary, barely there, resistance of bursting a wad of bubble gum with your finger as they passed through the Warped Mirror, then they stumbled forward onto their hands and knees, glancing around at the emporium.

"Did it work?" Sheed said, hopping to his feet, gasping like he'd run there instead of taking a couple of short steps.

"It did." Missus Nedraw stepped through the glass, and her reflection rippled for several seconds before settling.

The frame was different now. No longer the cheap wood with the clown painting. On this side the frame was dull aluminum, and their reflections weren't warped, just normal.

ENTRY #29

This frame is normal—dull, underwhelming—because it leads back to our world, which is normal—dull, underwhelming—to us.

DEDUCTION: All these mirrors lead to different emporiums in other strange worlds.

QUESTION: So why are we just now hearing about it?

Sheed scanned an aisle seemingly identical to what it was a moment ago. "How do you know we're here? This all looks exactly the same."

"As I said," Missus Nedraw began, taking the path back to the emporium's central hub, the boys following, "the emporium is the emporium. Beyond these walls, it's a different story."

Sheed said, "That sounds neat."

"It does, doesn't it? Now let's get those weapons you mentioned. How about a nice sharp sword?"

• • •

At the emporium weapons closet, an impressively deep, well-lit, and immaculately arranged armory locked behind a mirror that required a key card, access code, and retina scan to enter, Sheed did indeed pick a sword. It was a katana blade, similar to what samurai warriors wielded in his favorite movies. Otto settled on a nice slingshot with a pouch full of sterling silver ball bearings as ammunition. Missus Nedraw went for more variety, slipping a pair of bamboo escrima sticks into a pouch on her hip. She looped a bow and a quiver of arrows over her shoulder, and to round out her arsenal, the oddest weapon in the whole stockpile . . . a yo-yo.

"You any good with that thing?" Sheed asked.

Missus Nedraw flung the yo-yo at Sheed's face. He flinched, but the plastic butterfly wheel stopped an inch from his nose before it got snatched back on its string. The yo-yo smacked her palm, rebounding instantly as if her hand were made of rubber. Instead of angling for one of their faces again, it shot straight into the air while Missus Nedraw hooked its string with her other hand. In a series of quick, jerky motions, she'd doubled the string between her hands and made the yo-yo ride it up and down, up and down, like an elevator, before flicking her hands so the string coiled neatly around its spindle once more.

The boys' jaws unhinged.

"Pick your chins up off the floor. We have work to do."

Missus Nedraw led them toward the front of the emporium, barking instructions the whole way. "Listen up. What you're going to see beyond these doors will likely surprise you. There's no way for me to truly prepare you for what this world is without you actually experiencing it."

"Is it really bad?" Sheed asked.

"Horrible."

Otto, of course, had more questions. But something crunched beneath his sneaker, causing him to halt. Missus Nedraw and Sheed kept going toward the emporium exit just a few dozen yards ahead.

Otto lifted his sneaker, then knelt, examining the broken mirror shards he'd stepped on. "Missus Nedraw!"

"Young man, we do not have time to waste. Nevan and his gang—"

"I know, I know," Otto said, spotting more broken glass on the floor and a lot of empty mirror frames on various shelves. "It's just that you said the emporium doesn't change, no matter what world we're in. Right?"

Missus Nedraw's frown became more severe. "What are you getting at, child?"

"It's still a prison? The mirrors are cells?"

"Most are. Yes."

"Should we be concerned then," Otto said, "if there are a bunch of broken mirrors here?"

"Oh no," said the warden. "No, no, no, no no!"

She ripped an arrow from her quiver, nocked it, and drew the bowstring tight. Tilting her chin up, staring into the shadows overhead, she aimed.

Otto stared up too, as did Sheed, who said, "What are we looking for?"

"A gang."

"Nevan's?" asked Otto.

"No. This one is different."

Sheed said, "You sure do capture a lot of gangs."

Missus Nedraw said, "This one is called ArachnoBRObia. Very frightening. Very dangerous. Monsters!"

Something shifted in the inky gloom above them. Something not a shadow. Then something else. And more something elses. A dusky eruption of rapid movement from jerking, not-quite-right limbs, accompanied by skittering, scraping sounds across the ceiling. Plaster dust rained down and, with it, a drawn-out rasp. "Neeee-draaaaw."

Missus Nedraw's arrow swept back and forth as she attempted to trace the sound; it came from many directions, almost like a song. Sheed wielded his sword in a two-handed grip, while Otto plucked a ball bearing from his pouch, intending to load his slingshot—but something sticky and strong whipped from above and snagged his shooting hand. Before he could pull free, his other hand got snagged, then both his legs, and he was yanked from the ground and reeled up into the dark.

"Sheed!" Otto yelled.

Sheed came on the run, sword high, ready to chop through the binding strings. More strands flung from the dark, sticking his wrists together and snatching him off his feet as well.

The boys were dragged five, ten, fifteen feet in the air, and the closer they got to the ceiling, the more visible their attackers became. Though both boys kind of wished that wasn't the case.

Huge striped spiders with glowing yellow eyes and twitchy dripping fangs pulled them closer. Snagging them as easily as flies.

Everyone knew what spiders did to flies. Didn't they?

7

Tiny Meat People

SHEED HATED SPIDERS almost as much as he hated tentacles. Now he was developing a healthy dose of mirror hate, too. Though, with the speed that these spiders pulled him toward their eager mouths, he doubted there'd be much time for that mirror thing to matter.

The boys dangled high over the emporium floor, and while a drop from this height wouldn't have been pleasant, it was preferable to being eaten, Otto thought. He lurched toward Sheed, angling the webs holding him toward that razor-sharp sword. "Maneuver #8!"

Twist and shout! Sheed performed the maneuver, shifting his weight and shouting (because it's really hard to twist and not shout) just as Otto swung the webs holding his right leg and arm into the blade's path. The sword sliced the strands handily, freeing one half of Otto's body. While he couldn't accurately fire a slingshot with one arm and one leg, he could gather more momentum and swing faster toward Sheed's sword, angling just right . . .

A slice, and gravity. Otto fell, grabbing hold of Sheed's sneaker, saving himself from a nasty splat on the concrete below. Sheed could not slice his own bonds, so Otto began shimmying up his cousin's pants leg.

"You're going to pull my jeans off!" Sheed shouted.

"I hope you wore clean underwear, then."

"Maybe."

While Otto climbed, the air split as one of Missus Nedraw's arrows whizzed past his ear. The oblong arrowhead opened like an umbrella then expanded into a net, entangling one of the spiders. It fell from its ceiling perch in a writhing bundle.

"Broooo!" several of the spiders cried.

The one reeling the boys in didn't join the chorus. It said, "Don't worry, Tiny Meat People. I've got you."

Tiny Meat People? Oh, heck no. Otto shimmied faster.

Another arrow brought down another spider. If Missus Nedraw snared *their* spider in her net arrows, the boys might get hurt in the fall. Still, the spider's nest didn't exactly scream safety, either.

Otto climbed to Sheed's torso and grabbed his webbed wrists, twisting them in a way that let him work the sword's blade like a saw, splitting the sticky, tough material that held them suspended. They'd have to take their chances with the fall. Just . . . a few . . . more cuts.

The web snapped, and they were free. For a microsecond.

But a furry spider arm (hand?) grabbed Sheed's wrist and yanked the boys fully into the rafters. They each clung, terrified, to the narrow beam, eyeing the emporium floor far below.

"Well, mates," the massive spider said, lurching over them, upside down on the ceiling, "that was a close one. She almost got you. You're welcome, by the way."

Its words—and that it hadn't paralyzed them with venom and begun spinning them into a webby version of Grandma's Tupperware for later—confused Otto, made him forget his fear for a moment. "What are you talking about?"

"I'm Spencer. Me and m'brothers saved you. Right, fam?"

More glowing yellow spider eyes popped open in the shadows around them, like dozens of sunflowers suddenly blooming. Spencer's brothers murmured their agreement.

"Saved us?" Sheed said. "You don't mean for dinner?"

Spencer's fangs flailed, a gesture Otto somehow recognized as him being appalled. "What? Mate! No! Why would we—"

Another net arrow snared one Spencer's brothers, and that spider tumbled away.

"Oh. We should probably go." Spencer leapt nimbly off the ceiling, landing on the creaky beam, forcing yelps from Otto and Sheed. He grabbed each boy by the waist, tucked

46

them under a couple of his arms, and ran the length of the beam on his back legs, like a basketball player running a fast break.

Several of Missus Nedraw's arrows took down other spiders, but Spencer nimbly dodged them as they reached the end of the beam. The spider leapt high, snagged the flat ceiling with one of his sticky spider-hands, then swung his legs toward another section of the ceiling that popped up and out on a hinge, dousing them in bright sunshine. Spencer had kicked open a skylight with all of its glass panes painted black, and they were on the emporium's roof.

The spider's grip on Otto and Sheed did not relax as more of his brothers spilled from the open skylight. Dozens of huge, bigger-than-people spiders skittered onto the roof, like the horrific videos Otto sometimes showed Sheed on ThunkleTube, when a hundred baby spiders broke free of their egg sacs and erupted into the world. With some differences.

There were dozens here. Not hundreds.

They all wore clothes. Not in any sense the boys were used to — they'd never seen clothes tailored for giant, eight-legged individuals.

And the clothes were not flattering or stylish. What Otto had mistaken for natural color patterns on their fur and flesh were actually the black-and-white stripes of old-timey jail uniforms. Like in ancient movies Grandma sometimes showed them.

These jailbird spiders clustered around the skylight, cheering on their siblings. But the fortieth or fiftieth spider proved to be the unlucky one. A net arrow exploded from the skylight while he was halfway out, snagging him and pulling him back into the emporium.

"Brooo!" many of the spiders shouted, horrified.

A second arrow shot from the skylight. Prongs expanded from its head, turning it into a grappling hook, gripping the skylight's frame. Missus Nedraw was coming.

"Time to go," Spencer said, ready to run.

"Wait!" said Otto, "Put us down!"

"Yeah!" said Sheed. "You'll be able to get away faster."

As serious as the boys ever thought a spider could be, Spencer said, "That would mean leaving you here with that monster Nedraw. That ain't our way, mates."

And they were off.

Spencer and his brothers bounded across the rooftop with the heavy lumbering speed of fully padded football players. Leaping from the emporium to the slanted roof of the Lopsided Furniture Company, not slowing despite the extreme angle at which the roof canted.

Previously preoccupied with their captivity by a tribe of gigantic spiders, Otto and Sheed hadn't taken in their surroundings. Now, helpless to do anything but observe, they realized that they were getting their first exposure to the nature of the Warped World. For in the version of Fry that they'd come from, the Lopsided Furniture Company did not have a slanted roof (they were really committed to everything being level).

Spencer ran down the canted roof toward the next building, what should've been the Big Apple Bakery, which was no more than three stories high in Otto and Sheed's Fry. The building before them was twice as tall, and seemed to be rising slowly. Also, it seemed to be made of dough.

Otto looked to a wide-eyed Sheed, clutched in Spencer's other arm, his Afro pick bouncing with each of the spider's lumbering steps. "You seeing this?" Sheed said.

Otto could only nod.

Abruptly, Spencer changed direction, angling away from the bakery in favor of the edge of the furniture company's roof. He bounded off, into open air.

Everybody screamed! Otto and Sheed from terror, Spencer's shrieks . . . joyous. Otto thought all that worrying about Sheed was for nothing. *This* was how the Legendary Alston Boys of Logan County would end.

Spencer said, "Brace yourselves!"

He flipped midair, and thin arching strands of web shot out of him, snagging the corner of a building across the street. Their uncontrolled fall became a pendulum swing. They zoomed inches over the road, narrowly missing several Warped Fry residents out for a stroll as the arc of their

swing rocketed them up into weightlessness. At the peak of the swing, Spencer released his initial web and shot another. They were swinging again.

Behind them, Spencer's brothers performed a similar maneuver, one Otto couldn't help but number (#92 — Web-swinging), and beyond them, visible on the Rorrim Mirror Emporium rooftop, was Missus Nedraw in her archer's stance, arrow nocked, bow drawn tight. But Otto could tell they were well out of her range, and she knew it too. She let her string go slack, lowered her bow in defeat. That was the last Otto saw of her before Spencer swung them around a corner, deeper into this strange version of the town Otto and Sheed had known — or thought they knew — their whole lives.

8

Now We're Cooking

SPENCER DID NOT STOP SWINGING until they'd neared the other side of town.

Or what Sheed *thought* was the other side of town. Things were so different here; the landmarks he was used to were either too close, too far, or just plain wrong. Like the clock tower. It wasn't a clock. Or a tower.

It was a giant wristwatch.

Laid flat, the brown leather watchband stretched over two different roads, ticking loudly. The watch face was the size of a swimming pool.

Then there was the creepy old Machen House, with its spooky, dark gables, dangerous portal into the unknown, and consistent bat population . . . It was gone. You could see pipes and support beams poking from the ground, but it was like the house had lifted itself off its foundation and walked away.

It wasn't until they neared the park that Spencer finally touched ground and released the boys from his protective grasp.

"Whew!" he said, angling all eight of his eyes back the way they'd come. "That was close, wasn't it, fellas?"

His brothers dropped softly to the ground, surrounding Otto and Sheed. The boys had moved beyond the natural fear of the giant arachnids . . . They seemed sincere in their lack of hunger. A good thing, Otto supposed. Now what, though?

Beyond the park gate, children played on equipment similar to the playground in their world. The only odd thing was the kids looking in their direction at the group of huge prison-escapee spiders didn't seem fazed. Like nothing about this was strange at all.

This place was going to take some getting used to.

Otto did what he always did in stressful times, whipped out his notepad to scribble in while he talked. "You guys are the prisoners from the broken mirrors we found, aren't you?"

"Yes," said Spencer, motioning to himself with two arms covered in thick bristles. "You know me already. These are my brothers"—three arms waved toward the others—"Spaul, Speter, Spierre, the twins Spatrick and Spatrick Number Two, Spreston, Sp—"

Sheed interrupted the introductions. "Just want to clear something up here. You're not going to eat us? None of you?"

Spatrick and Spatrick Number Two had a suspicious gleam in their sixteen eyes.

Spencer said, "No." He turned to the twins and said it again, louder, for good measure. "No! We will not eat the Tiny Meat People."

"Otto and Sheed," Otto said, thinking it better the spiders stopped thinking of them as "meat people."

Spencer said, "We are fruitarians. We only eat fruit flies."

"That's not what fruitarian means," said Otto.

"Maybe not where you're from," Spencer said.

There was a rumble of agreement among the spiders. They nodded, flexed their fangs, gave high-fives that were more like high-forties when you considered the number of arms involved, though Otto didn't feel up for doing the exact math. Instead, he wrote.

ENTRY #30

Spencer and the other spiders seem friendly enough. They could've hurt us or—gulp—eaten us, but they haven't. So why did Missus Nedraw say they were dangerous? And why did they call her a monster?

DEDUCTION: Unclear. Missus Nedraw warned us Warped World could be

*illogical and unpredictable. Best to stay
on guard until we know more.*

While Otto wrapped up his Legendary Log entry, Spencer directed a question to Sheed. "So what they'd get you on?"

Sheed made a fish face, his mouth opening and closing with no sound escaping. Otto looked for gaps between the spiders in case they needed to make a run for it.

"Burglary, I bet," said one of the other spiders, maybe Spaul. "They're small, it'd be an easy sell."

"I don't know," said one of the Spatricks. "You see the way they got out of our webs? They're quick, a little sneaky-looking. I bet you could pin a con man rap on them easy."

Sheed, feeling defensive, found his words. "We're not con men or burglars! I'm getting really tired of people accusing us of stuff!"

Spencer laid a fuzzy arm on Sheed's shoulder, "Oh, we believe you, Tiny Meat Person. Just like we're not a gang. What you are, and what gets you stuck in a mirror, never really mattered much to the warden or the Judge. But all that's about to change!"

More murmurs and nods.

Otto said, "You *saved* us back there." He was only echoing Spencer's own words from the rooftop, unsure exactly what he meant. Best to say very little and let him fill in the blanks.

"Most certainly. When we saw Nedraw bringing you in, we couldn't let her imprison you. Nevan says we're going to need all of the help we can get. Even from tiny things like yourselves."

"Nevan the—" Sheed almost called him *the Nightmare* but felt the vibe was wrong here. "He freed you?"

"Of course! Then we freed you. We always pay it forward. It's only right."

Otto asked, "Do you know where Nevan is?"

"Yes! He's—"

Spatrick Number Two grabbed Spencer by the arms, his eyes narrowed suspiciously. "Stop talking, brother."

Uh-oh, Otto thought, *they know we weren't Missus Nedraw's prisoners.*

Sheed saw Otto tense. This might become a Maneuver #1 situation, and he was ready to run for it if need be.

Spencer said, "What's the matter?"

Spatrick Number Two's eyes bounced from Otto, to Sheed, then directly over Sheed's shoulder. "Fruit flies!"

The spiders looked beyond the boys at a tree that butted up against the wall around the park. Neither of the boys had noticed it before. Otto had the fleeting thought that maybe it wasn't *there* before . . . Warped World was so weird. But there it was now, and the boys were wary, wondering how big (and dangerous!) fruit flies were here. Considering the size of the spiders, the likely answer was *very!*

However, if there were flies present, they were stealthy things. There was fruit, sure, and plenty of it. No insects.

"What kind of tree is that?" Sheed asked. It looked like an apple tree, but the fruit was as bright and varied as a pack of Skittles. Reds, oranges, blues, pinks. Round, oval, oblong, banana-shaped. That a tree would have that many different things growing from it was perhaps another bit of Warped World strangeness.

"Careful," Spencer said to his brothers, who'd dropped low and skittered slowly toward the tree. "Careful."

A breeze sailed past, rustling the tree's leaves. Sheed saw a pink oval-shaped piece of fruit shake loose from its branch, bob momentarily on nearly see-through wings, then reattach itself to a different branch.

"Ohhhhh," Sheed said, getting it.

"What?" asked Otto.

Sheed was still irritated with the way Otto had been acting lately and felt no need to share what he and the spiders knew.

The fruit was the flies.

Spencer and the others were nearly close enough to leap into the tree branches. Spencer whispered, "Steady. Steady."

One of the Spatricks got a little too eager, leapt for a blue cucumber-shaped fly, and all the colorful creatures took flight like chunks of a shattered rainbow, escaping back toward town.

"That's lunch!" Spencer said, flipping into the air and

shooting his web, swinging in pursuit with all his brothers following.

"Wait. Please," Otto shouted after them, but they were too fast and too hungry to hear his pleas. They turned a corner, gone.

Otto and Sheed found themselves alone and dumbfounded outside the park gate.

Sheed backed against the fence and slid down onto his butt. His chest heaved like he couldn't catch his breath. Otto's worry meter shot to eleven. He knelt beside his cousin, his palm flattened on Sheed's chest. "Are you okay? Does your heart feel funny?"

Sheed smacked his hand away. "Giant! Spiders!"

Oh. This was a normal freak-out, not a health-related freak-out. Otto said, "In all fairness, they were very nice."

"I bet those fruit flies don't think so. What was all that about?"

Good question.

"Should we find Missus Nedraw now?"

Otto had thought about that, too. Considering what the spiders implied about the emporium, the warden, and the creepy Judge, he said, "Maybe we might do a bit of exploring for now. We can try to understand how this place works. Find our own answers."

Sheed gathered himself, breathing normally now, and faced the park where kids kept playing on swings, slides, and monkey bars. A little girl on the swing worked her legs, getting higher and higher, until at the peak of one swing, she jumped from her seat and kept going . . . away from the ground. She tumbled up, up, up, until she became lost in the too-bright sunshine.

Sheed pointed at the empty swing, descending in a series of shortening arcs until it was still. "Let's start there."

Entering the park felt normal. The gravel on the walking paths crunched under their sneakers, as usual. The grass was emerald green, with the alternating light-dark-light-dark rows where a lawnmower had recently done its thing, same as on the other side of the mirror. Some bigger Fry High School kids tossed a football back and forth. Then there were the kids closer to Otto and Sheed's age, who continued their playground adventures unbothered despite one of their number shooting into the stratosphere.

"Hey," Sheed said to no one in particular.

"Hey," a pale boy with hair the same light, almost invisible, color as his face said back. "Nice sword."

He wore a hoodie sweatshirt—lucky him, Otto and Sheed still wore the hot and itchy jackets and scarves Grandma had insisted on—and faded jeans. He played in the sandbox with his back to Otto and Sheed, his elbows pumping up and down as he worked on . . . something. His body blocked the boys' view of whatever project had his attention.

The moment the pale boy returned to his work, vague recognition lit up Otto's mind. He whispered, "Bryan?"

Sheed looked between Otto and Bryan, frowning. "No way."

This extremely pale boy bore a striking resemblance to one of Otto and Sheed's classmates, Bryan Donovan. Bryan was a quiet kid. He never answered questions in class, sat by himself at lunch, all but disappeared in the halls of D. Franklin Middle School. The big difference between the Bryan back on their side of the mirror and this Bryan was this one required a little more squinting, a little more head tilting.

They'd thought he was pale. Not so. Sure, he had a light complexion, but sandy would've been a better description. He was approximately the same shade as the sand in the sandbox. Even his clothes, though Sheed would've sworn they were a different color earlier. Now, if he shifted a certain way, he might not see Bryan at all. Kinda like an optical illusion.

"Bryan Donovan?" Sheed said. "That really you?"

Shuffling around, the boy kicked up a cloud that momentarily obscured him. The sand settled quickly, so Otto and Sheed were able to see his bright blue eyes and pearl white teeth. The rest of him was harder to track. He was very polite, though. "Do you guys need some help?"

Sheed said, "You don't recognize us?"

"No. Are you new in town? You look funny."

Otto and Sheed assessed each other, thinking they looked like their everyday selves, but whatever. Sheed said, "Yeah. We are new here. My name is Sheed. This is Otto."

Bryan chuckled. "That's funny. I go to school with a couple of guys who have the same names."

Otto's head tilted, and he fought a sudden panic. So there were an Otto and a Sheed here, but versions somehow different enough that Bryan couldn't recognize them, even though *they* recognized *him*.

What, exactly, do we look like here? Otto thought.

As someone who'd already met a different version of himself from the future, he wasn't eager to repeat the experience.

But Sheed's wide eyes and crooked grin suggested something different. "There's a him and me—I, I mean, an Otto and Sheed at your school?"

"Not today, silly. It's Saturday."

"Right." Sheed craned his neck, looking past the barely there Bryan. "What you doing in the box?"

"Oh, this." Bryan sidestepped to give the boys a glance at what he'd been working on. It took their breath away.

With a bucket of water and a plastic shovel, Sandy Bryan had built a spectacular sand sculpture. It appeared to be a house. A futuristic-looking one, all round and curvy, no corners. There was a yard, and bushes shaped like animals, and even tiny sand people standing by the front entrance waving at no one in particular.

Otto stepped forward, then stopped suddenly, afraid his heavy footfalls would topple the masterpiece. Sheed leaned into Otto, whispering, "I've seen Bryan—*our Bryan*—drawing in a sketchbook sometimes. Not a lot of people know he's a really good artist."

"More like an architect," Otto whispered back.

Sandy Bryan tweaked an edge on his creation, unbothered by their side conversation.

Some observations . . . connections . . . deductions began to form for Otto, but he needed more information. "Bryan, what happened to the girl who jumped off the swing into the sky?"

"You mean Maddie? She's going to be an astronaut."

It wasn't quite the answer Otto expected, but it was enough to draw conclusions. To Sheed, he said, "That was Madison Baptiste. Our version is always talking about going into space."

"I know. She's the only one in science class who gets grades as good as Wiki and Leen. So, here, she can fly?"

"I don't think it's that simple. It was more like she . . . *launched*." He whipped out his pad, trying to make sense of what might not ever be made sense of.

ENTRY #31

Personality seems to have some sort
of physical effect on the people and

places here. Madison Baptiste is smart enough to be an astronaut, so she zooms into the sky. Bryan Donovan is shy, so he blends in with the sand.

DEDUCTION: I think we're in for a lot more surprises today.

Sheed rotated in place, taking in their surroundings fully. Otto followed his lead, seeking more strangeness. The Fry High kids throwing the football . . . The one with the best and most accurate throws appeared to have a mechanical arm. The one who made the flashiest catches had huge hands with webbing between the fingers. A man and woman sat on a blanket with a picnic basket between them. The woman's face was huge, and red, and heart shaped. It appeared to pulse slightly. The man's face was slender, tapered; light reflected off slivers of blue crystals—ice!—embedded in his skin. The picnic basket shuddered and bounced like something living was trapped inside.

"Look!" Sheed said, pointing across the grassy expanse.

They saw the first familiar, and not-warped, sight they'd experienced since coming through the mirror. It was Mr. James, the kind man who loved to barbecue in the park and feed anyone around his perfectly roasted hot dogs, juicy hamburgers, and sticky saucy ribs (Otto's favorite).

"Bryan," Sheed said, "we'll be right back."

The boys jogged across the park as they'd done many times on their side of the mirror. "Mr. James! Mr. James!" they yelled, and waved.

He'd been dragging his big, heavy soot-covered grill behind him with one hand, and his huge red and white cooler full of meats, and spices, and sauces with the other hand, like always. He set it all down in his usual grilling spot before greeting them. "Hey, there, you two."

Still friendly, probably still willing to feed them. That was Mr. James. But, unlike *their* Mr. James, there was a glossiness in his eyes that was not recognition. Like Sandy Bryan, the grill master didn't know them in this world.

Fear and frustration swirled together then washed over Otto in a dark wave. Sheed felt tired. Like he'd finally reached a level of strange so extreme, it just wore him out even thinking on it.

Even if Mr. James didn't recognize them, it was some comfort to know he'd still bust his grill out and cook for the residents of this mirror world. This place couldn't be all bad.

"Sir," Otto said, "do you need any help setting up?"

"That would be mighty fine of you, young man." His face was the same. His voice was the same. His politeness was the same.

"What do you need us to do?" Sheed asked.

"Well, if you want to grab some steaks from that there cooler, that'd be mighty helpful."

Sheed popped the lid on the plastic bin and found slabs

of red meat wrapped in wax paper, separated by several ice packs. He scooped up two of the biggest. "Where would you like them?"

"Right on the grill, son."

This . . . was odd. The grill was cold. There was no charcoal, or propane tank like Otto was used to seeing. He could tell from Sheed's frown that he was thinking the same thing. But an adult they respected had told them to do something. Sheed followed the direction and set the two steaks on scorched, but cold, grill grates.

"Good, good," Mr. James said. "Time to cook. Stand back."

Otto and Sheed took two big steps back, still unsure about where the necessary heat would come from. They saw no matches. Not even one of those clicky torch things that looked a little like a ray gun but spat a tiny flame from its nozzle.

"One," Mr. James said, "two . . ."

Otto heard "three" in his head, though he never heard it come from Mr. James's mouth.

The explosion was too loud.

"Whoa!!" The boys scrambled backwards, shielding their eyes with their hands, blinking away the red and orange spots that crowded their vision.

The worst kind of fear ever smacked the boys, as they thought they'd witnessed the tragic end to their friend Mr.

James. A massive wall of swirling orange-white flame occupied the place where he'd stood just moments before. It seemed to have consumed him.

Then he whistled. "Whew! That's what I'm talking about. Getting a nice char on it."

The flames hadn't consumed Mr. James.

He. Was. The. Flames.

His fiery hands hovered over the steaks that curled and blackened in the intense heat. Mr. James stared at them with eyes like lava, his white-hot metal smile wide inside the wicking flames engulfing his head. "You boys look cold. Should I warm you up a bit?"

Otto and Sheed sprinted away, no maneuver consultation needed.

They ran in the direction of the sandbox where Bryan stood knee-deep—a depth that really shouldn't have been possible in the shallow play area. He saw them coming, waved one of his sandy hands, and said, "Sorry, fellas, gotta go. Mom's got lunch."

He sank into the sand as if being tugged down slowly by some unseen force. Horrified, they whipped toward the Fry High kids. The makeshift quarterback no longer had a mechanical arm; he was mechanical everything. A for-real throwing machine with his pronged feet fastened to the ground by bolts. His receiver had become some sort of frogman, snatching tossed balls from the air with his tongue. The couple on the blanket . . . There wasn't a couple. The icy man was nowhere in sight, and the woman with the heart-shaped face now had a jagged crack running down the center of her forehead while she sobbed into her hands.

In nearly every direction some horrible strangeness confronted the boys. They ran down the straight gravel path, legs pumping, arms arching, toward the park's exit. The path whipped left, then right, became a writhing snake beneath them as the entire landscape shifted from flat to hilly. Still, the exit drew near. Otto and Sheed threw themselves beyond the park's border, twisting back to watch the landscape ripple, rise, fall, swirl . . . all motions that might have seemed okay at a beach if they were watching the ocean's waves. Land shouldn't be this fluid. This unpredict-able. This . . . *warped.*

The boys rose and ran some more, with no destination in mind. Hearts pounded. Beneath their feet the Warped World rumbled, as if it had a big beating heart of its own.

9

The Spuds Have Eyes

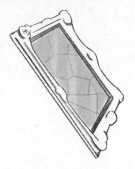

"IT'S LOCKED!" SHEED SAID, tugging on the big brass handles at the Rorrim Mirror Emporium's entrance. "Missus Nedraw! Hello!"

Otto cupped his hands around his eyes to block the sunlight, and pressed his forehead against the glass but detected no movement inside the gloomy prison. He backed off and peered down Main Street. "She's probably out looking for us."

"Or that Nevan guy and his gang," Sheed said.

"She needed our help for that."

"Now that you've seen this place, do you feel helpful?"

Sheed had a point. It had taken some doing to make it back to the emporium, because the streets had changed. The avenues and intersections no longer matched the Fry that the boys were used to. Missus Nedraw wasn't kidding about this place being unpredictable. Thankfully, east, west, north, and south seemed to still be in the right places, so a little trial and error while still moving in the same general directions got them where they needed to go.

"Should we just wait here?" Sheed sounded skeptical. Main Street was not deserted, after all. Warped World residents churned along on the sidewalks and flitted in and out of the other shops. What few there were.

That was a huge difference between their world and this one. Where their Main Street was home to longstanding Fry businesses, many of the shops here were closed, the interiors dark from desertion, or the windows covered with sheets of wood. On each of those unoccupied storefronts was an ominous flyer pasted to the door that read

CLOSED UNTIL FURTHER NOTICE DUE TO
UNLAWFULNESS

Beneath the vague proclamation was an emblem that appeared to be an ornate frame—like the kind you'd find around a mirror—and at the center of that frame, an open eye, always watching.

The sign bothered Otto a lot, though he didn't spend much time contemplating it with various Warped World residents roaming about. At a distance, they might look like people the boys were used to seeing any Saturday, but the closer they got, the more the Warped effect became clear.

One woman with a big purse looped over her arm

looked totally average, until she turned sideways, revealing she was flat. A two-dimensional person, like a living sheet of paper. She purchased a ticket at the movie theater's box office, then slid inside through a slim crack between the door and door frame.

An elderly gentleman who walked with a cane seemed tiny in the distance. As he got closer, he should've seemed bigger. The opposite happened. The closer he got, the tinier he became, and by the time he trotted by Otto and Sheed, his cane tap-tap-tapping with every other step, he was the size of a sparrow.

All sorts of things like that happened around them, and the residents seemed unbothered.

As disturbing as the skewed reality of the place was, more disturbing was what the residents did seem to be noticing.

Otto and Sheed. With their puffy winter coats when it really wasn't so cold—thanks, Grandma—Sheed's sword, and Otto's slingshot wedged in his belt.

They did not present like all of the other Warped World residents. While Sandy Bryan and Fire Mr. James greeted the boys' otherworldliness with kindness, others scrutinized the boys in uncomfortable ways.

Otto said, "I don't think we should stay here."

"Where we going, though?"

Good question.

Finding Missus Nedraw seemed the logical course of

action, but where to start? If they were looking for her and she was looking for them, but in all the wrong places, they could spend the entire day missing each other. No telling what might happen in the meantime.

Especially if Nevan the Nightmare was really as bad as she claimed.

Sheed offered up a solution. "We could go find us—I mean, this world's version of us."

"No!" Otto shouted, angry and scared at once.

Sheed flinched. "Whoa, Otto. What was that?"

Otto scrambled for a satisfactory answer. "Think of all the comics we read. Meeting other versions of yourself rarely goes well." Which he knew, from experience, was sorta true.

Sheed chewed his bottom lip, looked at—*through*—Otto, like he was a code that needed cracking. Finally, he said, "Fine. We still need to talk to someone we can trust here."

"Like?"

Sheed's lips curled into a grin. "I know who."

Otto felt like he'd stepped in a trap. "Sheed . . ."

Sheed left the cover of the emporium awning, angling in the general direction of where the Fry Pavilion should be. "Follow me."

Otto yelled back, "Where?"

"The farmer's market."

• • •

Otto added more entries to his log. Most were mundane observations—that weird mirror/eye flyer on the closed shops they'd passed, the surprising shapes and sizes of the residents out and about—things scribbled simply to help him calm down. But he finally got to his thoughts on Sheed and the barely missed land mine of going to visit the Warped World versions of themselves.

ENTRY #44

I shouldn't have gotten angry about Sheed wanting to find us. If I hadn't met TimeStar on the last day of summer, I might've been excited about meeting us, too. Just seems to me that only weird and horrible things happen when you start talking to your-self. Seeing yourself different.

DEDUCTION: We need to finish our business here quick, fast, and in a hurry. As Grandma would say.

When Otto glanced up from his pad, Sheed—whom he'd caught watching him—glanced quickly away.

It was a short walk north from the emporium to the Fry Pavilion, where the farmer's market took place every

Saturday—a tradition that had hopefully been maintained in this alternate universe. The closer they got to the pavilion, the more Otto's stomach churned as he worried about the possibilities of what a farmer's market might be like here. They heard the haggling chatter of the shoppers and sellers, a buzzing similar to a beehive.

Please don't let there be actual giant bees, Sheed thought while mentally preparing himself for just that.

Cresting the hill and getting their first full glance at the farmer's market, there did not seem to be actual giant bees. It all looked like what they were used to. As did the emporium and the park. At first.

Sheed reached over his shoulder, grazed his sword's pommel, comforted knowing it was still there. Otto dipped his fingers into the pouch on his belt, still loaded with smooth metal ball bearings for his slingshot.

A wide parking lot separated the boys from the vendors. They weaved around cars that varied between overly large, like limousines, but without the tinted glass, to too small, like toys. As they moved, some of the long cars snapped to a more reasonable size, while some of the smaller cars inflated, bulging against the neighboring cars with a lurching screech of metal on metal.

The boys sped up, fearing they'd get caught between two expanding cars and crushed, and they were flat out sprinting by the time they reached the seller tables.

There were people at the market, but the crowd was

way thinner than it would be back home. There were fewer vendors, too. While everyone chatted, bustled, made their selections, and paid their agreed-upon prices, it all felt diminished when compared to the boys were used to. The people moved with their eyes cast down and their shoulders slumped. Frightened, like animals before a storm.

Sheed also noticed the wide variety of physical differences on display. There were extended limbs, bulbous heads, animal ears, and people made, apparently, of glass. The boys moved into the crowd without making eye contact, in search of the table Sheed had come for, hoping it wasn't so different they wouldn't recognize it.

Some tables they passed were familiar. The potato farmer, Mr. Hannamaker, was there, looking much like himself. Though his potato bushels were unsettling since the potatoes had eyes. Not the usual little dents and divots, mind you. These potatoes *had real eyes* . . . the blinking kind.

The boys kept moving.

The Pepperling family's table was set, and their colorful peppers, always bright as candy, arranged the way Otto and Sheed were used to, though the hot peppers smoked and radiated waves of heat like asphalt in the summer.

The boys kept moving.

Pastries were made from actual paste and came from orange-tipped bottles like the kind they squeezed glue from in school. They watched a lady squeeze several croissants right into her canvas shopping sack. Homemade jams were large, bouncing musical symbols — treble clefs and half notes — that lurched and vibrated inside of sealed mason jars that *clinked* when they bopped into each other. And so on.

Sheed pointed, his hand shaking with nerves. "There, I see them."

Otto spotted what had to be Ellison's CORNucopia — the table Wiki and Leen worked with their uncle Percy every weekend. Sheed braced himself. There was no telling what this world's Epic Ellisons would be like.

They shuffled to the CORNucopia, only to find an unmanned table. The bushels were there, brimming with corn. There were cornbread squares individually wrapped in cellophane. Cornmeal in poofy brown bags. Corn tortillas. And — in the center of it all, super odd — a computer monitor. No Ellisons.

Sheed said, "Where are Wiki and Leen?"

"I'm right here."

The boys leapt backwards, bumping into some passersby, who shot them annoyed looks but kept moving. Otto scanned the area, trying to track Wiki Ellison's voice. The computer monitor on the CORNucopia table blinked on, giving a high-definition view of Wiki's perpetually frowning face. "And who might you be?"

The boys stared at the monitor. Otto, still operating

on nonwarped logic, searched for cables snaking from it to some camera broadcasting from Wiki's actual location.

The monitor rose. It had been sitting behind the table, not on it. And, really, not sitting, since it appeared to be mounted atop a neck, which sat between two thin shoulders, above a sternum that was covered by a D. Franklin Middle School sweatshirt.

"Oh wow!" Sheed said. "You're Wiki."

The monitor tilted and the projection of Wiki's face glitched, a jiggling line of static scrolling from the top of the monitor to the bottom. She said, "You're Otto and Sheed Alston, but not the ones from around here."

Sheed said, "How do you know that?"

Otto, always irrationally irritated around Wiki, waved the question off. "The three thousand similarities in our faces or something. Doesn't matter. Where's Leen?"

Beside Wiki's monitor head, the very air split. It was a slow unzipping, as two delicate brown hands widened the gap, first revealing long white sleeves, then familiar short, springy hair with dark goggles on her head. Leen Ellison wriggled out of—well, Otto didn't know what she was coming out of.

The air bunched like cloth as Leen worked her chest free, then her stomach, until she'd wiggled the mass of invisible stuff down to her thighs, then stepped from the whatever-the-what like Grandma stepping out of her big, yellow galoshes.

This Leen wore a full-length white lab coat, a dark shirt, and dark necktie. Tiny tendrils of lightning sparked between the short, curly hairs atop her head. The whispers of her mad scientist ways never seemed more accurate than they did here.

To Wiki, Leen said, "See? I told you my reactive camouflage sack works. Makes me dang near invisible."

"I still don't think it was a good idea to test the new version on yourself. Not after what happened to that monkey."

"You promised you wouldn't bring up the monkey again!" Leen tipped her chin to the sky and laughed maniacally.

"Ummm," Sheed said, "hey, Leen."

Her head jerked his way, and she snatched her goggles

from her scalp to her eyes. Sheed couldn't see anything through the black lenses but guessed that wasn't the case for her.

"Who are you supposed to be?" she asked.

"Otto and Sheed Alston. From some other dimension," said Wiki.

Leen scoffed. "No way. Sheed is much cuter than that."

Sheed's shoulders slumped. Otto patted his back comfortingly.

Leen's black lenses panned up and down the boys. "Maybe." Her voice went up an octave, excited. "Then that means . . ."

Wiki sighed, "Parallel dimensions are real."

Leen pumped a fist. "Yes! Pay up."

Wiki fished a dollar from her jeans and handed it over.

Before they could get off on another tangent, Otto said, "Since that's settled and you know we're Otto and Sheed, we were—" This part felt like chewing glass, but: "hoping you might help us."

"Otto Alston," Wiki said, "is willfully requesting assistance from the Epic Ellisons? You really are from another world." She motioned to her side of the CORNucopia table. "Step into our office, and we'll figure out how to save you this time."

10

An Epic Sale

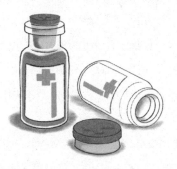

OTTO AND SHEED PERCHED on two stools behind the CORNucopia table. The Ellisons insisted the boys take their seats because, according to Wiki, they "looked like they needed a break."

Otto referred to his notes and recapped all that had happened since the morning began. The girls became more attentive, their faces more serious, when he described the true purpose of the mirror emporium. When he finished, Computer Head Wiki waved Mad Scientist Leen over to the far end of the table to confer in hushed tones.

Sheed leaned into Otto. "What's up with them?"

Otto shrugged.

The girls returned, and Wiki said, "As much as it pains me to admit it, you've provided us with critical information we haven't been able to gather on our own."

Otto could barely contain his glee. "Go on. Tell us more."

Wiki's monitor face glitched momentarily, becoming static filled and irritated before returning to her previous, high-definition display. "That emporium 'opened'"—she made air quotes with her fingers signaling sarcasm—"here a little over a year ago, same as in your world. That was right around the time things started going bad in Logan County."

She let that hang. Otto scribbled down notes while Leen tapped a button on a high-tech silver gauntlet that ran from her wrist to her elbow. A translucent blue lens swung from her hair on a mechanical arm and hovered just over her left eye. She angled the mysterious monocle toward Sheed, examining him and mumbling, "So not cute."

Sheed sulked.

Otto peered up from his pad and said, "Bad how?"

Wiki said, "People disappearing. Mayor Ahmed announcing all sorts of new laws while looking scared all the time. We found the timing suspicious because that emporium just kind of showed up. It was always locked, even during its posted business hours. We tried more . . . *creative* ways to sneak inside, but nothing worked."

Leen, still scrutinizing Sheed with her high-tech monocle, grumbled, "We didn't try explosives."

"No," Wiki said, stern, "and we never will."

Leen groaned.

"We tried ladders, lockpicks, grappling hooks, and glass cutters." Wiki shook her monitor head. "Something's wrong with the windows and doors. Like they're paintings of windows and doors instead of the real thing. Which makes no sense."

"Magic," Sheed said. "Also, a lot of stuff around here doesn't make sense."

"Says who?" Wiki said.

Leen tilted closer to Sheed before he could answer, her monocle flickering with analysis only she could see. She frowned. "Are you feeling okay, Less-Cute Sheed?"

"He feels fine," Otto snapped, afraid of what that fancy monocle might be revealing.

Wiki said, "This Missus Nedraw, we've seen her. On a couple of occasions when we were watching the emporium, trying to figure a way in, she'd pop up out of a side door with a wagon full of mirrors that she'd walk around downtown Fry."

"She was letting the prisoners get some sun," Sheed explained.

Wiki said, "And you think we don't make sense."

Otto tried to keep them all focused. "Why do you think the emporium had something to do with people disappearing?"

"Have you seen the closed shops downtown?"

"Yes."

"Those shop owners were the first to disappear. Their

businesses are sealed with that creepy mirror-eye emblem. It doesn't take a deductive mind like mine to connect those dots, though I can understand why you might have a hard time seeing it."

"I did see it!" Otto insisted.

"Sure, Otto."

He jabbed a finger at her. "Wiki Ellison, you are . . . not nice!"

Sheed shook his head. "Not everything is different here."

Leen said, "If the emporium's a prison, it stands to reason that the missing Fry residents are trapped inside. In one of those cell mirrors."

Wiki said, "Sound deduction, sis."

"We should probably do something about that."

Otto had been making lots of journal entries, but found this new information troubling.

ENTRY #52

First the spiders, now this world's
Wiki and Leen are indicating Missus
Nedraw is shady, and the emporium
isn't being used to contain "gangs" and
"monsters" like we were led to believe.
Has Missus Nedraw been lying to us?
She doesn't <u>feel</u> like a liar. She's a

little intense, but everyone makes her sound like a bad guy. We've seen a lot of bad guys, and she doesn't seem like them at all.

(POSSIBLE) DEDUCTION: Maybe very good liars have a way of making you feel okay about them.

"Hmmm," Leen said, looking deep down the row of merchants, her monocle shifting from blue to red, "that's strange and likely not a coincidence. Missus Nedraw is here."

The boys hopped off their stools, peering through the crowd. "I don't see her," Otto said.

Leen tapped her monocle. "That's because I'm looking *through* everyone. Her and the other guy are, like, fifty yards away."

"What other guy?" asked Sheed.

"Don't know." Leen punched some buttons on her gauntlet, "I've never seen him before, but his bones are incredibly dense. Must be very strong. Be tough to get a saw through those."

"What does he look like?" Otto asked, deliberately ignoring Leen's comments about sawing through bones.

"It's a little hard to tell when I'm scanning his body for

parts—er, I mean, for *anomalies* like this. We all mostly look the same on the inside."

Wiki said, "Just zoom out, sis."

A few more taps on the gauntlet. Then, "Tall, flappy robe, greasy hair, and a really big mallet."

"Not a mallet," Otto said. "A gavel."

The Judge was here.

Sheed said, "This is one of those 'it's good we saw them before they saw us' situations, right, cuz?"

"I gotta agree with you there." The boys searched the CORNucopia booth, panicky. Time was running out.

Wiki sighed heavily. "You're trying to figure a way to execute Maneuver #2, aren't you?"

Leen tapped her gauntlet. "You two really are so lucky to have us."

Otto and Sheed hugged each other tightly. It was the only way to fit inside the camouflage-cloaking-invisibility-sack-thingy of Leen's. She got them zipped up tight, so they felt like the stuffing rolled into a big old burrito, and Otto was convinced the device didn't work. The material felt as light and thin as silk, thin enough that the boys could still see through it to all that was happening around them. So, surely, anyone looking in their direction would see the two brown boys, frozen in an awkward embrace, inside of a weird sack. Right?

Shoppers continued passing the CORNucopia, sparing glances for nothing but the ears, meal, and bread the Ellisons sold. If anyone did raise an eye in Otto and Sheed's general direction, it was as if they looked right through the boys at something well beyond them.

"Don't fart," Sheed whispered, shifting slightly in the tight space.

"You're the one who farts when you're nervous."

"I was talking to myself. Now, shhhhhh! I'm concentrating."

Missus Nedraw led the Judge through the market like a loyal guide. But a closer look—something most of the wary shoppers weren't willing to do, as they simply flicked frightened glances at the towering menace that was the Judge —made it obvious that while he gripped his long-handled gavel in one hand, the other clamped down hard, perhaps painfully, on Missus Nedraw's shoulder.

She still carried her bow and quiver and escrima sticks and yo-yo, yet she seemed far from the imposing warrior they'd first seen in action on the last day of summer.

In addition to his giant gavel was the leather book with the yellowed pages he'd been holding when the boys first saw him in the mirror. It hung from the Judge's hip in a wide holster. From this distance, Otto made out six embossed letters stamped in the book's spine. It read: THE LAW.

They moved at a steady pace, and just when it seemed they might pass the CORNucopia altogether, Missus Nedraw slowed.

Otto's heart knocked around his chest. He gasped, nearly gagged, and whispered to Sheed, "Concentrate harder."

Sheed was too nervous. He did the only thing he thought was fair, and whispered back, "You should probably pinch your nose."

The Judge, his mouth hidden behind the long strands of black, greasy hair, spoke with a voice like crunching gravel. "Why are you stopping?"

Missus Nedraw, voice quaking, said, "Nevan the Nightmare loves corn. He may have been drawn this way."

"For your sake, I hope that is true."

"Judge, I'm sorry I —"

"Lied to me? Used one of my mirrors to cross into" — he nearly snarled — "*this unruly place?* As if I wouldn't know."

The quaking in Missus Nedraw's voice became something like irritation. "Well, I was unaware you monitored mirror travel so closely, since I'm supposed to be the one in charge of the emporium." For a moment she became the stern and scary warden Otto and Sheed had come to know.

A brief moment.

"HOW DARE YOU SPEAK TO ME IN SUCH A MANNER, EVIAN NEDRAW!"

The entire farmer's market froze as the Judge loomed

over her, the head of his gavel glowing with ominous purple energy. Missus Nedraw's fists were clenched at her sides, and she held his gaze longer than anyone would've considered reasonable. But eventually, she flinched. The denizens of the market resumed their previous activities —though for many their new priority was to get the heck away from there. The thin crowd became thinner.

The Judge said, "You are only free now because I don't have a suitable replacement for you. Yet. You'd be wise to use this time to atone for your negligence. Find. Nevan."

She broke free and approached the CORNucopia table. The Judge trailed.

Leen remained professional, despite the terrifying nature of these new customers. "Could I interest you in some of our finest pickings? A whole bushel would only cost you five bucks."

The Judge's eyes were hidden by the hair falling over his face, but his head angled Leen's way. He said, "That price seems . . . excessive. Maybe even illegal?"

"Illegal?" Wiki said. "You try hauling those bushels from the truck while Uncle Percy naps in the passenger seat. Trust me, it's a bargain."

The Judge chuckled. It was the kind of laugh you hoped to never hear if you walked past a cemetery at night. "You make a sound argument that aligns with the Law." He patted the book dangling from his hip. "Compensation *should* match effort. Good for you. No punishment today."

"Punishment?" Wiki tensed. "Who are you again, Mister?"

The Judge had lost interest in the Ellisons, directing his comment to Missus Nedraw. "Have you found any clues?"

"No." Missus Nedraw examined a bushel closely, frowning and squinting. "Perhaps these girls have seen something?"

Missus Nedraw slid a hand beneath the lapel of her suit coat, freeing a folded piece of paper. She flattened it on the table. A WANTED poster.

"Young ladies, have you seen this individual? He may have been toting about a dozen mirrors."

Only then did it occur to the boys that they didn't have a clue what Nevan the Nightmare looked like.

Wiki and Leen reviewed the poster. Sheed got more nervous. Otto pinched his nose harder.

The Judge lifted his gavel, then slammed the butt of its handle onto the ground, creating a thunderous clap that drew yelps from nearby shoppers. "Have. You. Seen. Him?"

Wiki and Leen, still as tough and defiant as the boys knew them to be, answered.

Leen said, "We . . ."

"Have not," finished Wiki.

The Judge released Missus Nedraw's shoulder, snatched the WANTED poster off the CORNucopia table, held it high for all to see. "Has anyone seen this dastardly fugitive? Speak up! And allow me to remind you that withholding information or aiding this monster in any way is a clear violation of THE LAW! Anyone caught in violation of THE LAW will be tried and sentenced at my discretion."

Nervous murmurs rippled through the farmer's market, but no one spoke up.

The Judge crumpled the WANTED poster and shoved it into the folds of his robe. "Let's go. We're wasting time."

"In a moment." Missus Nedraw reached into her coat again, producing a slim purse this time. She set it on the CORNucopia table, opened its wide top, and rummaged around inside with both hands.

"What is this?" the Judge sniped. "What are you doing?"

"Compensation should match effort, as you said. These girls tried to help us, and it appears we've scared off any other potential customers. I'm buying a bushel."

His pale chin angled at Missus Nedraw, then the Ellisons, then back to Missus Nedraw. "The Law is the law, I suppose. Fine. But hurry."

Missus Nedraw still rummaged in her purse. It didn't seem big enough for her money to be that hard to find. Otto risked unpinching his nose so he could get a better look, but before he could, she produced a folded bill and pushed it into Leen's palm. "Thank you."

"You're wel—"

Missus Nedraw snatched up the nearest bushel and strolled quickly away, dragging the Judge along with her.

When they were long gone, Leen unzipped the

camouflage sack. Otto gulped greedy mouthfuls of fresh air, while Sheed said, "Warned you."

Wiki led an oxygen-deprived Otto back to his stool. Leen unfolded the money Missus Nedraw handed her. "I think this is for you two."

She dropped two things into Otto's palm. A small brass key and the five-dollar bill it had been folded into.

On the creased bill, there was a message written in small, hasty letters:

O&S, Thank you for trying. Consider the slate wiped. This key will get you into the emporium. Go there. Go home. Before this world changes you. —Missus Nedraw

Sheed read over Otto's shoulder. "She knew we were here?"

"Or knew Wiki and Leen would be able to get this to us."

"She's telling us to run home. So she's not threatening to throw you in a mirror anymore."

"I don't think so." Otto should've felt relieved. But . . .

"She's in trouble." Sheed said.

Otto said, "We're not going to take this key and go, are we?"

Wiki shook her head. "Even I know the answer to that."

11

The Beat Really IS Sick, Though

LEEN LEFT WIKI MANNING the CORNucopia while she escorted the boys through the parking lot. Because the Ellisons were longtime participants at the farmer's market, they knew the paths between cars that wouldn't get you crushed as vehicles warped into different shapes and sizes.

Otto appreciated the escort and not getting crushed, but he was less comfortable with the way Leen kept giving Sheed up-and-down looks with her sees-through-people monocle. Could she see whatever secret sickness lurked in his bones and blood? Would she reveal the hidden knowledge Otto had clung to so tightly since the last day of summer?

"Take a left at that brown station wagon," Leen instructed, and Sheed obeyed. "Now right at that red truck."

Otto, hoping to distract Leen from Sheed, said, "Isn't it scary how things change so suddenly here? It's all so weird."

Leen came to a sudden stop, miffed. "Things aren't weird in the Logan County you come from?"

Otto said, "Yeah, but—"

"But nothing! You have your weird, we have ours. You shouldn't turn your nose up because the place you go isn't like the place you been," Leen said, swinging them around the fender of a sports car—the tires were soccer balls.

Otto felt a little embarrassed and put out. Very much like when Grandma corrected him for something he probably should've known better than to say or do.

They reached the end of the lot. Beyond it, an open field pocked with dips, hills, and shrubbery extended to the north toward the Fry border.

Leen said, "If you guys want to get back to town, circle west. Should keep you clear of Missus Nedraw and that Judge guy."

"Thanks, Leen," said Sheed.

Otto begrudgingly said, "Should we need an assist?"

"Me and Wiki are done with CORNucopia duties in, like, two hours. If you survive until then, we'll look for you."

"If we don't survive?"

Leen smiled wide and scary. "I'll still look for you. Can't let good parts go to waste. Good luck." Her eyes bounced between them. "Or not."

She weaved her way back to the market, leaving the boys alone. Otto was relieved she didn't say anything to tip

Sheed off to his illness. Sheed was relieved the Leen back home never talked about using people for spare parts.

"We gotta get outta here," they said together.

They continued north a ways before swinging west, to be sure they weren't spotted. It gave them time to think, plan.

Sheed said, "This isn't right, Otto. First Missus Nedraw is all 'Help or you're going in a mirror!' then she's like, 'Go home, you're free.' Which would be awesome if it didn't seem super obvious she was in trouble with the Judge."

"We don't *know* she's in trouble."

Sheed's expression scalded him. "For real?"

"We don't know."

Sheed exploded then, in typical Sheed fashion, words rushing from him like the steaming whistle from a teapot. "If you're scared, just say you're scared! Are you?"

"No." Yes. Yes, he was. But not of the Judge. Well, maybe he was a little scared of him, but that wasn't what made him quiver most.

Sheed said, "Whatever is up with you, it's been going on for weeks, and I'm sick of it."

"You're sick," Otto said, testing the words but unable to stop there, still reluctant to tell the whole truth in the moment, "of . . . what?" His own anger was rising.

"Of you acting like a . . . a . . ."

"Acting like a what?"

Sheed got fully in his face then. "Like you're not a legend."

That stung.

Otto shoved Sheed. "Take it back."

Sheed laughed. Loud. At the sky. "That's all you got? Stop acting all scared and . . . and *soft* . . . and I will."

Scared and soft? *I'm acting like this for you, dummy!* Otto thought, just about vibrating with rage. He veered away from Sheed, still moving in the same general direction as him, but also apart. "Don't talk to me right now."

"Gladly!"

Otto resorted to his Legend Log, drafting several nonsensical entries that were really just his way of releasing his fury quietly.

ENTRY #WHATEVER

I'M SCARED?! SOFT?!

SOFT!!!!!!

BIG DEDUCTION: Sheed. IS. STUPID!

He burned through a few more pages, most expressing the same sentiment over and over, while Sheed walked slightly ahead, swinging his sword at nothing in particular. Not paying Otto any mind. Or pretending not to. Jerk.

Otto kept writing mean things about him, even going for words that Grandma would've washed his mouth with soap over if she knew he knew such language. As far as he was concerned, Sheed deserved every one of them. Otto was so mad, he was ready to vocalize some of the nastiness he'd scribbled down. Only when he glanced up again, Sheed was nowhere in sight.

"Sheed?" he called, still mad, though the anger gave way quickly to his finely tuned sense of *something ain't right here.* The tiny little hairs on the back of Otto's neck stood up. He pocketed his notepad and drew his slingshot, quickly loading a ball bearing into the shooting pad. He tugged the rubber bands taut and turned in a circle, ready for whatever danger was near. "Sheed, where'd you go?"

He sensed the subtle vibration at his feet a second too late.

There was a slight, earthy breeze. A flap of grass flew back like the top on Mr. Green's old-timey convertible cars. Four arms snatched Otto backwards and down before the flap resealed, blocking all the sunlight.

Otto OOFED! when he crashed to the cavern floor. The sudden dark was alarming, and cold, and Otto nearly screamed when he sensed the inhuman, yet familiar, scurrying all around him. Before he freaked out, a hand touched his shoulder, and Sheed said, "We're cool. I think. See?"

And Otto could see, the cavern was not totally dark,

thanks to a few lit torches revealing the spider brothers
—and some other new acquaintances—surrounding the
boys.

Spencer stepped forward, six of his arms spread wide
for a hug. "Hey there, buddy." He scooped Otto up in an
embrace, his coarse spider hair as comforting as pine nee-
dles. "It's been a minute."

Otto squeezed Spencer's thorax lightly, just so he'd let
go, then dropped to the cavern floor at the huge spider's
feet. "What is this place? How'd we get down here?"

"Oh, that'd be m'cousin, Spenelope. Say hi, Spenelope."

"Hey," said a slender, slightly shorter giant spider, also
in jailhouse garb.

Spencer said, "Her thing is trapdoors. And beats."

"Sick beats, mate." Three of her spider hands cupped her
twitching mandibles, and she began to beatbox.

A-BOOM-BOOM-BAH-DAP-DAP-BAH!

All around, Spencer's brothers, cousins, or whatever
began gyrating, spinning, doing flips into handstands. And,
clearly forgetting the uncertainty of the situation, Sheed
joined in with his own popping-and-locking . . . until Otto
popped him in the back of the head.

"What?" Sheed said, perplexed. "The beat *is* sick."

"Enough!"

It's what Otto felt like saying, though he wasn't the one
who said it. He doubted he could've pulled it off with that

much authority. Spenelope stopped beatboxing. The other spiders stopped dancing. Then they parted, allowing a much tinier creature to hop through.

He came to Otto's belly button. Was furry, with perky ears, a pointed snout, and a beard like Santa Claus. The toes of elongated patent-leather shoes extended past the hem of his small billowing black robe, and a thick tail swished from the back. He looked very much like a small kangaroo. He said, "State your names."

Cautiously, Otto introduced them. "I'm Otto. He's Sheed."

Sheed's chin tilted. "Who are you supposed to be?"

The creature's eyes narrowed. "My name is Nevan."

"The Nightmare?" Sheed smacked his forehead, realizing he probably shouldn't have said that part.

Nevan seemed unphased. "No. I'm Nevan *the Judge*. I mean to take my title back."

12

Kangaroo Court

"HOW CAN YOU BE A JUDGE when you're a—" Otto almost said *monster*, Missus Nedraw's word, but it felt rude saying it to Nevan's face like that. "A prisoner at the emporium?"

Nevan spread his arms. "Do I look imprisoned?"

He did not. Especially given the various adornments that Otto had overlooked upon their initial introduction. His stubby fingers poked through several thick gold rings dotted with colorful jewels. More gold peeked over the collar of his robe, the links in a chain leading to a diamond-encrusted medallion resting on his chest. His front buckteeth were gold. He reminded Otto of Grandma's cousin Rufus, who wasn't a judge. Rufus was a truck driver.

Sheed said, "Missus Nedraw told us—"

"Evian Nedraw is sorely mistaken on many things. What else has she told you?"

Otto spoke plainly. "She said you're the leader of a gang."

"A gang!" The tiny creature threw his hands up, his jewels winking reflected torchlight, then hopped around the cavern. "Oh Evie, Evie, Evie. Go on!"

Otto motioned to Spencer and Spenelope. "She said they're part of a gang, too. I think she called them—" He flipped through his notes. "ArachnoBRObia."

Spencer laughed in a horrific way that made his mandibles jiggle and drip saliva. "We're no gang. We're a dance crew."

"The best dance crew," Spenelope confirmed. "But I never liked the name. I'm not a bro."

"I told you to give us some suggestions for a better name."

"I did. The Spinsters. It's inclusive, with layers. But we went and got locked in mirrors before the crew could vote."

"Well, then it's just a matter of patience. We're out now, the monthly meeting is still on the third Wednesday. We'll add it to the agenda and—"

Sheed cleared his throat loudly, interrupting. "If you're not a gang, why'd you get locked up in those mirrors?"

Nevan's authoritative voice became sheepish, embarrassed. "That would be my fault."

Several spiders grumbled or sighed. Spencer placed a comforting hand on Nevan's shoulder. "Don't beat yourself up, mate. We all got caught up in that crazy unfair system. And you got us out. That means a lot."

Nevan paced the cavern floor. "I know. I know. I did manage to free us all from our horrible circumstances, didn't I? A bit of a hero I am. That does count for something. But I can never be truly free of blame."

"Why?" Otto asked.

"Because the whole Mirror Prison System," Nevan said. "I created it."

The Legendary Alston Boys leaned in. This they had to hear.

Nevan swept a hand across the entire expanse of the cavern. "This place we're in now, this strange, strange world—it is not the world any of us originate from. My eight-legged friends have a home away from here, as do I." He motioned to Otto and Sheed. "As do you, I presume."

The boys nodded.

"And you understand how vastly different these places can be?"

Yes. After today, Otto and Sheed totally understood.

"Where I come from, there are strict laws that help make our society comfortable for all. When people broke such laws, they came to my courtroom to have their fate decided."

Sheed said, "So, like, if they robbed a bank or something?"

"Well, yes. That would fall under criminal law. We covered the other laws as well. Like civil law. Or the law of gravity. Murphy's law—"

Sheed made a T with his hands. "Time-out. How can someone break the law of gravity?"

Nevan looked aghast. "Oh, you would not believe the depths some will sink to. There was this lawless family back home. Absolutely *depraved*. They invented a machine meant to lift people off the ground for extended periods of time, then lower them back to earth at a location well beyond where they could've leapt to with their own legs. Insanity, I tell you. It was one of the easiest decisions of my career. If they never get out of their mirrors it will be for the best."

Otto lowered his notepad, startled. "The machine, it had wings?"

"Yes."

"This depraved family, was it a pair of brothers?"

Nevan went wide-eyed. "You've heard of the case, then?"

Sheed, his face fixed in a disbelieving frown, recalled what they'd learned about this particular family and their machine at school. "You're talking about the Wright brothers?"

As in the inventors of the airplane and the fathers of modern aviation. At least in Otto and Sheed's world.

A creature with the head of deer and gold chains coiled around his antlers—presumably a member of Nevan's "gang"—said, "More like the *Wrong* brothers."

Nevan chuckled at that one, as did the rest of his associates. The spiders looked as uncomfortable as Otto and Sheed felt.

Sheed said, "YOU LOCKED UP THE WRIGHT BROTHERS?!"

Nevan's eyes narrowed, and the cavern became a few degrees cooler. "They broke the law. Wasn't I clear about that?"

Otto touched Sheed's sleeve, signaling for him to back off. "We get it. You enforced laws where you come from. Where did the mirrors come in, and how you'd end up in one?"

Nevan calmed, but Otto noticed his robe seemed tighter somehow. Like it had shrunk in that moment of irritation.

Or he'd grown.

He said, "We have always used mirrors in multiple ways. Communication. Short-range travel that's much more civilized than—*blech*—flying. And, obviously, interdimensional travel between parallel earths."

Sheed mumbled from the side of his mouth, low enough for Otto to hear, "Because no way that breaks any laws."

Otto elbowed him in the ribs to shut him up.

Nevan went on. "But we'd locked up so many disobedients that our prisons were stuffed to capacity. It occurred to me and my colleagues that there might be yet another use for some specially constructed mirrors. For the space it took to house one prisoner in a conventional cell, we could keep twenty or thirty in a single mirror cell of my own design. And we could store a thousand mirror cells in the same space it takes to keep a hundred prisoners. Don't you see how marvelous that is?"

Nevan's glee over this admission chilled the boys.

Otto looked to one sleepy-eyed, sort of adorable figure standing just over Nevan's shoulder. She wore a flower print dress and looked like a sloth. If sloths were also rappers. Because she was rocking a serious platinum chain encrusted with emeralds. "What do you have to do with all this?"

She motioned with her long sloth fingernails (painted red to match her lipstick) in the direction of the other strange and bejeweled individuals. "We're the Jury."

Otto scribbled and mumbled, "Judge. And jury."

"What's up with the other Judge, then?" asked Sheed. "Why's Missus Nedraw working for him if it was your system?"

Irritated, Nevan returned, "He's no Judge. *I'm* the true Judge. My loyal friends here are my Jury. And that *usurper* was in my employ as well before he betrayed me."

Otto said, "He worked for you. As what?"

"My Executioner," Nevan said. "Of course."

"What?!" Sheed said. "That big, diesel, zombie-looking dude kills people?"

Nevan stuck one hand out, held it flat, then made a back-and-forth waffling motion. "Eh."

"Eh. What's eh?"

"We didn't, exactly, ever sentence anyone to death. We're not barbarians. So, while the Executioner was around if needed, he was never, *actually*, needed."

Otto said, "He had a job he never ever did? For how long?"

Nevan was hesitant, but did answer. "Roughly eight hundred years or so."

Otto gawked; he looked to the Jurors. "Were you guys there the whole time?"

A tall, slim Juror that resembled a rabbit in a breezy tropical shirt with gold doubloons falling out of his stuffed pockets, said, "Jury duty is a big time commitment."

"A civil responsibility," Nevan corrected.

Otto became steadily unnerved. "I can understand a world where the laws are very strict. Our grandma, and our friend Leen, I guess, say different places and people can have another way of doing things, and we should respect those differences, but how did this mirror system end up in their world"—he pointed to Spencer and the spiders—"or our world, or here in Warped World?"

Nevan stroked his chin and shook his head slowly. Obviously saddened. Or wanting to appear that way. "Once word of how efficient my system is got out to the most powerful people in the various dimensions, there was little to be done to keep this innovative and cost-saving technology from rapid expansion."

"Yes, yes. Rapid expansion. The investors insisted on it," said a Hippo-like Juror with a big mouth and a sapphire nose ring.

The cutting look Nevan gave him suggested the boys weren't the only ones who thought that Juror had a big mouth.

"You got paid," Sheed said, sneering, "to lock people up in your mirrors."

ENTRY #60

Nevan and his Jurors invented the mirror cells and got rich (or got a really good deal on their jewelry)

106

selling the idea to all sorts of different worlds. I guess that makes sense,
but . . .

Should people be able to get rich
locking other people up? Especially
over laws that feel unfair? As Sheed
said, THEY LOCKED UP THE WRIGHT
BROTHERS!

DEDUCTION: Missus Nedraw had her own
reasons for calling Nevan a nightmare,
but now that I've met him, I think the
name fits perfectly. So what are me
and Sheed going to do about it?

"What are you writing there?" Nevan asked, suddenly
at Otto's hip. This close, he looked different. Before, Otto
thought he was a few inches shorter, more round than muscular. Not so. Now he was almost as tall as Otto, and the
muscles in his arms and chest bulged through the fabric of
his robe.

Otto flipped his notepad closed and said, "Nothing."

Nevan huffed. "At least you're using a pencil. That's the
right way to do it. In case you make mistakes. Use of per-
manent ink is strictly forbidden where I'm from. Unless you
apply for a proper permit."

"Do the permits cost money?" Sheed's eyes were narrowed.

"There is a small fee, payable to the court," Nevan confirmed.

A Juror with a face like a koala bear held up a golden cup embedded with gems. "Permit fees bought me goblet!"

Sheed turned his displeased gaze on Spencer and his crew. "Where do you fit into this?"

Nevan spoke before Spencer could. "They were wrongly imprisoned by that so-called Judge and Evie Nedraw. Just like me and my Jury."

Spencer's head bounced. "Yeah, mate. Like, ten years ago. We were dancing to protest the shenanigans of this big company that was trying to tear down our webs so they could build a factory. Things were going good, then someone sprayed us with some sort of knockout gas. When we woke up, we was in one of them mirror cells."

"And I'm so sorry that happened to you," Nevan insisted. "Had I still been running the show, there was no way a peaceful protest like yours would've resulted in incarceration."

Otto's pad was open again. He rushed to write this all down. More information led to more questions. Like why did Missus Nedraw's boss betray Nevan? But as he began to ask, screams from the shadowy recesses of the cavern broke his concentration.

13

A Stone Cold Punchin'

"Ow, ow, ow!"

"Who is that?" Sheed said, so done with surprises. His hand brushed the hilt of his sword.

Spencer said, "Oh, that's Spablo. He broke three of his arms escaping the emporium, but the doc's fixing him right up."

Otto's ears perked at the D-word. "There's a doctor here?"

"Hold still!" said another voice. It sounded familiar.

Otto and Sheed wedged between the spiders and crossed into another chamber, where a squirming Spablo did not hold still despite the prodding of someone in a long white coat.

The boys only saw her in profile and were at first confused because she had the head of a dark brown Labrador. Her glasses, voice, and determination were the same as they knew from back home, though. Traits as clear as the name on her clinic door. Together, they said, "Dr. Medina?"

Her doggy head tilted, curious. "Do we know each other?"

She didn't recognize them. Same as Wiki and Leen and Bryan and Mr. James. Sheed was more curious than ever about what this world's versions of them actually looked like.

Otto was uninterested in another conversation explaining where they'd come from and how they'd gotten there, so he simply said, "We've heard good things about you."

"Well," she said, "you haven't caught me on my best day." Her snout angled toward a broken vial resting in a bright yellow puddle on the cavern floor. She turned her attention to the writhing Spablo. "Thankfully, I brought a spare."

A crowd—spiders, Judge, Jurors—gathered at Otto's and Sheed's backs, watching the doctor work.

Her medical bag sat at her feet; she reached inside and produced another tiny bottle of glowing yellow liquid that made Otto think of a funny combination of words: *Lemon Ink.*

The doctor uncorked the bottle and gave Spablo a determined look.

"It's going to taste bad!" Spablo scooted into a corner, as far as the cavern allowed.

"Bad taste versus broken bones. There's really no decision to be made here," Dr. Medina said.

Spablo cradled his three arms, bent at wrong angles, to his thorax. "It's gross!"

"Open your mouth right now, young spider!" said Dr. Medina.

Otto had somehow gained the ability to recognize what spider pouting looked like. Spablo spread his mandibles, and Dr. Medina poured the bright yellow solution down his throat. "All done."

Otto didn't believe she was all done. Because when Stan Bander from their school broke his arm trying, and failing, to climb the sign outside the FISHto's fast food restaurant, he needed a cast. Spablo should need at least three casts.

Or not.

Spablo's fear switched to curious awe, his eight eyes staring at his misdirected limbs. The lowest arm twitched, then corrected its angle with a quick snap that made everyone in the cavern wince. Followed by the next highest arm. And the next. Within seconds of Dr. Medina administering that dose of Lemon Ink, the spider's broken arms had righted themselves.

"No way," Sheed said.

"That's . . . incredible," said Otto, his total focus shifting between Dr. Medina's medical bag and that empty bottle the solution had come in. Just drinking it *healed broken bones* (or whatever Spiders had)!

What else could it do?

What else could it *cure?*

Otto's gaze shifted to Sheed, who knew nothing of the illness lurking in his body.

Maybe he never had to.

Spencer slipped arms over Otto's and Sheed's shoulders, ushering them back to the main cavern. Otto kept twisting his neck, not wanting to let Dr. Medina's bag out of his sight.

"My work is done here, but I'm always on call for the resistance." Dr. Medina asked Spenelope, "Could you let me out, please?"

The beatboxing spider skittered to the cavern ceiling and unlatched a flap Otto hadn't noticed until that very moment. A concealed rope ladder dropped from the exit's edge, and Dr. Medina gathered her things.

"Wait!" Otto said.

Everyone looked his way.

"Ummmmm . . ."

"What are you doing?" Sheed said, his face scrunched while picking his 'fro.

"It's just—she's a doctor."

Sheed nodded slowly, some quiet decision made. He wedged his pick tight in his hair. "I would apologize in advance for this, but, for real, you've had it coming."

"Had what—"

Sheed punched Otto in the shoulder. Hard.

There was a solid *THUNK!* as Sheed's fist connected.

Otto winced at the pain he anticipated, but it . . . didn't . . . actually . . . hurt.

Unexpectedly, Sheed's face creased with the sudden pain he *hadn't* anticipated. He slowly retracted his fist, stared at his knuckles, and let out an echoing "owwwww!"

Dr. Medina had only climbed a few rungs on the rope ladder. She leapt down, her doggy eyes curious. "What's this, now?"

Sheed angled his fist toward her. "Something's wrong with my knuckles. See?"

The doctor examined the flesh. "Slight bruising. Not unusual."

"It is when I'm punching him."

Dr. Medina regarded Otto, his shoulder specifically. She squeezed his muscle, a sensation he barely felt. "Interesting. Remove your coat, please."

Otto felt nervous and self-conscious with so many eyes on him — since the spiders had eight eyes each, it was especially nerve-racking. He did as told, afraid the doctor would instruct him to peel off his shirt next. He'd only shaken his coat off one arm when the doctor held up a halting hand. "That explains it." She pressed her glasses higher on her snout. "You're turning to stone."

The boys gaped, but Spencer wiped fake sweat from his brow with two arms. "Whew. And here I thought it was something serious."

14

The Scent of Cranberries

OTTO TRIED NOT TO HYPERVENTILATE over the gray cracked granite covering his arm (or was it his actual skin now? ACK!) from the hem of his shirtsleeve down to his elbow. It hadn't overtaken his hand, but given where Sheed punched him, he knew the rocky spread had reached his shoulder and was possibly creeping toward his neck.

Double ACK!!

"Why"—Otto fought to keep his voice steady—"am I turning to stone, Dr. Medina?"

"Why are your eyes brown? I did not come down here to give lectures on basic biology."

"Doc," Sheed said, "I don't think turning to stone is part of basic anything."

"What medical school did you attend?"

Sheed's mouth snapped shut.

Dr. Medina said, definitively, "This is a routine physical fluctuation, is all. It will pass with time."

Otto said, "That's good to know."

"Or it will get worse."

"That's not very encouraging."

"I'm not here to encourage you. I'm in this moist, mildewy hole to fix a serious injury so this plucky band of rebels can keep fighting and ensure the tyrant who's been disappearing members of my community is dealt with. Isn't that right, Nevan?"

She peered over the lenses of her glasses with chocolate eyes, waiting.

Nevan said, "We will take care of my former Executioner, and you will be handsomely rewarded for choosing the right side of this fight."

"Getting my friends and neighbors back is the only reward I'm concerned with. Let me know if you need any more help."

Dr. Medina returned to the ladder, to Otto's dismay. He wanted to know more. Not just about his *physical fluctuation*, but the extent of the fantastic medicine available in this world.

Spenelope thanked the doctor again and ushered her up into the world above, while Spencer said, "Nevan, mate, what's our next play? How we gonna make sure the fake-Judge-Executioner guy don't hurt nobody else?"

Nevan, who now seemed slightly wider than he had a moment before, said, "By giving him a little of what he's been dishing out. Real justice. The right justice. We're going to throw him in a mirror for the rest of eternity."

That snatched Sheed's attention. "Wait. What?"

Nevan's eyebrow arched up. "Is that a problem?"

"I mean, he seems like a bad guy. But eternity is a long time. And what you're saying doesn't sound like justice. It sounds like revenge."

"It's only right."

That word again. Right. Right. Right. But how did Nevan *know* that was the right thing to do?

There was a screeching tear of ripped fabric. Nevan puffed up like dough from a biscuit can and gained a few more inches, swelling right before Sheed's eyes. The bigger, stronger Nevan—now almost Sheed's height—bounded toward Sheed with heavy bounces. "I'm not sensing a strong commitment to handling our predicament the right way."

The Jurors and the spiders gathered at Nevan's back, chins and mandibles high, troops in the presence of a great general. Sheed stood his ground, though his legs felt only slightly steadier than jelly. In times like this, maybe he wasn't the best spokesman for the Legendary Alston Boys of Logan County. He turned to Otto. "What do you think about all this?"

Except Otto wasn't there.

• • •

"Dr. Medina, wait up." Otto padded away from the cavern flap, following the doctor toward town. She did not wait up, or even glance in his direction.

So Otto sprinted. Or tried to. His stone arm was heavy; it made him lean to one side and lope awkwardly. He eventually caught her, matching her pace.

She sighed. "Let me guess. More questions."

"I have some."

"Before you start, my first answer is I'm a veterinarian."

"I, uh, okay."

"That means I'm an animal doctor. You are not an animal."

"But, back there —"

"Yes, I gave a quick assessment of your physical fluctuation because you appeared to be part of the resistance. However, since you're chasing me and not actually resisting, it seems you're more selfish than I assumed, and I'm no longer inclined to help."

Otto, in a flash of rage, grabbed Dr. Median's coattail, yanked, and yelled, "I am not selfish! If only you knew."

Dr. Medina's doggy nostrils flared. Her eyes narrowed. A low growl rumbled in her chest.

Otto released her coat.

"No, selfish you are not. What I smell on you is . . . desperation. Your questions aren't about you, are they?"

He was unsure of how much he wanted to say, or even think about, for fear of his traitorous smell giving away more than he wanted to reveal. "What does desperation smell like?"

"Cranberries."

"Oh."

"I do need to return to my office and check on my patients. Feel free to tag along. I am now open to further conversation, you intriguing and strange creature."

"Um, thanks."

They continued trekking toward town.

"He's going to notice you're gone," Dr. Medina said. "This is about your friend with the fantastic hair, isn't it?"

"He's my cousin. His hair isn't that fantastic."

She sniffed. "That's not jealousy. You love him, and you're trying to downplay it."

"That smell thing is creepy."

"Not creepier than some of the actual smells around here. Trust me." She shuddered.

Otto wasn't so much concerned with smells as he was with what he'd say to Sheed when they met again. Sheed would notice he'd left the cavern, and that would require an explanation whenever they reconnected. Otto wouldn't be able to keep the possibility of Sheed's impending death from him much longer.

That was how important this gamble was, because if what Otto suspected was true and the miracle medicine of the Warped World could indeed cure Sheed *before he even got sick*, then whatever happened after didn't matter. He'd gladly explain what he'd learned on the last day of summer, why he'd kept it secret, and how he wasn't sorry. Because Sheed would live.

"That medicine in your bag—the Lemon Ink—how does it work?"

"Lemon Ink? You mean my supply of Fixityall. It works like all medicine here. Great."

"No, I mean—"

"I know what you mean. Unless you want to enroll in several years of medical school, I will explain this as succinctly as I can, and you can try to understand without interrupting. Deal?"

119

"Deal."

"You're not from here. I can smell that on you, too. Where you're from is of little concern to me. Here, this world, is my concern. I have to tell you this is—or was— a lovely place to be. We eradicated any sort of significant disease a long, long time ago. Maintaining the health of those who live here is more about treating surprise injuries, of which there are quite a lot. Like your spider friend's broken arms."

"But *you* didn't fix his arms."

"You're interrupting."

"I'm sorry, but you *didn't* fix them. He drank that stuff, and the arms fixed themselves."

Dr. Medina nodded, her snout bouncing up and down like the needle on a finicky gauge. "The compound I gave your spider friend is an old remedy that strengthens the body against all known sicknesses, injuries, contusions, and/or scrapes. Largely, we don't need medicine, but in the occasions when someone gets hurt or, heaven forbid, gets *sick*, it resets the body to a completely healthy state."

"That's for *any* sickness?"

"That we know of. What does your cousin suffer from?"

Otto watched his shoes as he walked. "I don't know for sure. I just know it's bad."

"It must be. I can smell that, too."

"Would you stop with the smells!"

Dr. Medina huffed. "So you want to know if the medicine of my world can stop a sickness from yours."

"Yes."

"That is an iffy proposition." She motioned to Otto's stony arm. "You see for yourself that the body works differently here than what you seem accustomed to."

Understatement, Otto thought.

"But it's possible, perhaps even likely, that our medicine would help your cousin. How long do you plan to be here?"

"Ummmm, not long."

"Well then, that's our biggest problem."

"Why?"

"Because if your cousin isn't going to stay here forever, I cannot provide treatment. It would be bad for everyone." She sped up, separating from Otto and speaking over her shoulder. "Safe travels."

15

Dance Break

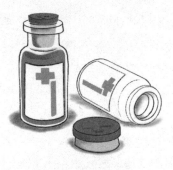

SHEED SPUN IN A SLOW CIRCLE, checking the shadows, in case Otto was still there but had gone full Rock Man and was just being really still. But he was nowhere to be found.

"Did you see him leave?" Sheed asked Spencer.

The spider shrugged all six of his shoulders.

"Did you?"

A significantly bigger, beefier Nevan shook his (still tiny) head. "Well, isn't that strange?" His voice was deeper, more befitting his expanding body. "Why would your buddy run off like that?"

"He's my cousin, and how should I know?"

Nevan scowled at Spencer. "You said the two of them were Evie Nedraw's prisoners?"

"Yep. We saved them right after you freed us."

"Were they restrained? Did she have mirrors prepped and ready to confine them?"

Spencer's mandibles twitched. "Well, now that you mention it, I don't think so."

Uh-oh, Sheed thought.

In the adjacent cavern, Spenelope rolled up the rope ladder the doctor—and probably Otto—had used to leave the cavern. She was oblivious to the increasingly tense conversation, bobbing her head rhythmically, lost in thought.

Sheed yelled, "Spenelope!"

"Yeah, mate?"

"Let me hear your sickest beat!"

She didn't even hesitate. She dropped the end of the ladder so it unrolled and dangled, then began beatboxing . . .

DO-DO-BUM-BUM-BAH-BUM—

The spiders, unable to resist, began dancing in earnest. The arachnids took up all the available space, moving in time with Spenelope's music. It became hard to see what was what and who was who.

Nevan saw through the scheme immediately. "Stop! Stop it! It's a trick!"

He swelled even more with anger—shoved through the undeterred dancers. He grabbed Spenelope, pinning her arms to her sides. The sudden silence halted all movement in the cavern.

Except for the rope ladder, which swung wildly from Sheed's hurried escape.

• • •

Maneuver #57 — misdirection!

Upon emerging from the trapdoor, Sheed spotted a small hill to his left, the direction he and Otto had been heading in when they were first snatched underground. He unsheathed the katana blade he'd been carrying and flung it as hard as he could so it landed halfway up the hill, the blade piercing the earth.

Then, spotting a patch of shrubbery to his right, he ran for the bushes and leapt behind them, peeking between the leaves.

Those he'd left underground spilled out, led by Nevan (who could barely squeeze through the trapdoor he was so swollen with new muscles). Spencer followed, then the rest. Nevan caught sunlight glinting off Sheed's discarded blade and pointed. "That way!"

Nevan, the spiders, and the Jurors rushed up the hill, where Nevan grabbed the sword, turned it end over end, then snapped the blade like a twig before flinging the broken pieces aside. "Those boys were spies. We have to catch them before they report back to Evie Nedraw and her Executioner master! They could bring down our entire resistance if we don't do something."

Spencer scratched his head with two of his right arms. "They didn't seem like very good spies, mate."

Nevan grew another three inches, yelling, "Because you're not looking at it the right way!"

The entire group flinched. Nevan waved a fist toward town. "Let's go! He couldn't have gotten far."

The bunch of them disappeared over the hill. Good news for the moment, but following the quickest, most direct route into town meant following them. A dangerous move when Sheed was still vastly outnumbered by Nevan, the Jurors, and the spiders. Best to hang back a bit. Play it safe. But . . .

If they got to Otto before he did, there was no telling what they'd do to him. Sheed's emotions swirled in a big old ball of scared and mad. He was almost certain Otto had run after Dr. Medina because he'd been all-doctors-everything lately.

Why, though? Why abandon me to do it? Think, think, think.

He could go south to the farmer's market and get more help from Wiki and Leen, but that would mean navigating that parking lot with the scary expanding bumper cars. He'd most likely be splatted before he got anywhere close to the CORNucopia.

Turning east, Sheed spotted the crest of what seemed a familiar chunk of land—though you could never really tell in this wacky, shifting place. If he was right, that was Harkness Hill. And between Harkness Hill and Fry . . . was Grandma's house.

What . . . if . . . ?

Otto would have a fit, and Sheed was nervous because everything was so different here, yet who better to get him out of a jam than the Legendary Alston Boys of this particularly warped Logan County?

Otto and Sheed helped people. Surely that wouldn't be so different here.

With his mind made up and his heart pattering with low-key excitement, Sheed set off to meet, well, himself.

He swiped his Afro pick through his hair, Mad Scientist Leen's little digs about his looks fresh in his mind. He mumbled, "I bet he isn't that much cuter."

16
Who's a Good Wolverine?

THOUGH DR. MEDINA DIDN'T SPARE HIM another glance after wishing him a safe trip home without the medicine that might save Sheed's life, Otto lumbered on behind her. The rocky casing overtaking his flesh had spread across his chest to his other shoulder, making him heavier and heavier; still he labored on. He had to.

The animal hospital was next to the *Logan County Gazette* office, just like in Otto's version of Fry. Unlike home, the newspaper office was made from actual newspaper and spontaneously folded in on itself, creating a new alley between it and the vet's place. Dr. Medina was unfazed, undoing her lock, triggering the door chimes, and flipping on the ceiling lights in the reception area.

Otto followed her in, and that low growl rumbled in her chest again. "You're still here."

"I am."

She continued through the reception area into the treatment rooms at the back of the building. As did Otto. While she made no effort to stop him, he was greeted by a volley of barks, meows, quacks, clucks, howls, and hisses.

The room was lined with cages where sick and healing animals rested on cushy pads with food trays and water bowls in easy reach. The doctor walked the perimeter of the room, eyeballing and sniffing her patients.

Mostly, they looked like the kind of animals he was used to. Exotic, yes, but recognizable. There were some fur and plumage variations he found surprising—the cat covered in brown feathers, for example, or the fluorescent blue baby bat—but mostly this all seemed what an animal hospital should be.

"All appear to be doing nicely," Dr. Medina said, kneeling by the final, and largest, enclosure, which held a—

Otto gulped.

It was that wolverine. Well, not the exact wolverine that seemed ready to tear a chunk out of him back home earlier, because that wolverine was still on the other side of the mirror. This Warped World wolverine was the green of tropical birds. Its claws and teeth were pink. It seemed the sort of colors that would glow neon under the cool black-light bulb he and Sheed had back in their bedroom.

Dr. Medina poked a hand in the wolverine's cage, stroking its head. It twisted its muzzle toward her fast. Otto flinched, expecting the worst. It only licked her fingers.

"Good girl," Dr. Medina said.

Something occurred to Otto, a welcome distraction, since the wolverine craned her neck his way, her purple eyes pinning him. "Doctor, the way the buildings sometimes shrink and expand—aren't you worried that would hurt the animals? Or us?"

She shook her head. "We adjust. That's what life is. You either adjust or you're not around very long. Either way, the problem is solved."

That sounded grim.

"You didn't keep following me here to discuss the ins and outs of oscillating architecture."

"Osci-what?"

Dr. Medina sighed heavily. "I already told you helping your cousin might be a possibility if he were willing to stay. To administer the sort of medicine we use here without that guarantee would be irresponsible. There could be extreme side effects."

"Like what?" Otto said. "They can't be worse than Sheed *dying*."

"You would think that." She shuddered so strongly, her doggy ears flapped even after the rest of her stopped.

Otto was appalled. "You don't know, though. It might be risky, but it's a risk I'm willing to take."

"That is obvious. But is he?"

"I—" Otto's mouth snapped shut.

Dr. Medina's nostrils flared. She shook her head. "He

doesn't know about his condition. This hardly seems the sort of thing you should know when he doesn't."

"It's complicated." Otto's leg itched; he felt stoniness creeping down his thigh. Perhaps he should've been alarmed, but he was more concerned about the accusatory tone in the doctor's voice.

"My point is if he stayed here, I could monitor him and make sure the medicine did more good than harm. To put that medicine in him and let you cross back over into your world"—another head-shaking, ear-flapping refusal—"I can't do it. It's irresponsible. Dangerous in ways neither of us can possibly understand. I'm sorry."

"It doesn't feel like you're sorry." Otto tugged his notepad from his pocket, finding it a little hard to manage because some of his fingers had become rocky, too.

Dr. Medina threw up her hands, conversation over, then disappeared into a back room to rustle through supplies. That was fine; Otto didn't like how the conversation had gone either. Not one bit.

ENTRY #61

Dr. Medina is being stubborn. She doesn't get that anything to save Sheed is worth the risk. If it was someone she cared about, like one of these animals, she'd definitely get it.

DEDUCTION: *I don't have time to convince her.*

Especially when there were more vials of the glowing miracle medicine Fixityall in a cabinet that was uncomfortably close to the green wolverine.

Dr. Medina emerged moments later, finding Otto, his notepad closed and put away, in the same spot he'd occupied when she'd entered her supply closet. Bundles of bandages and ointments were cradled in her arms. She tossed a tube of something to him. He caught it, read the label: FLUX-SPORIN. Half of that name made him shiver with bad memories of his and Sheed's summer foe, Mr. Flux.

"Rub some on your stone bits. It'll help with the physical fluctuation."

Otto said, "This will give me my skin back?"

"No. That's ridiculous. It will help make sure the rock doesn't chip off and leave pebbles everywhere. No messes."

You are a terrible doctor, Otto thought. He said, "Are you sure there's nothing we can do about my arms?"

"I swear, I don't know what sort of backwards, primitive medical science they have in your world, but I will explain this condition as best I can. Physical fluctuations happen when there's a shift in your body, physical or mental. You have to think thoughts that aren't rocky and hard."

"I don't know what that means."

131

She got frustrated. "It's like we're speaking different languages."

"Yes. It is!"

A shrill ringing tore the air, drawing Dr. Medina to a telephone mounted on the wall. Otto's relief over a device that seemed to work the same way here as at home was overwhelming.

Then Dr. Medina ripped the entire phone from the wall and tossed it aside. The plastic box clattered end over end across the animal hospital floor, the bell inside clanging sporadically from the impact, startling Otto while the animals remained calm and on the mend.

"Hello? How can I help you?" Dr. Medina yelled at the frayed wires protruding from the wall.

From the bare wires, another yelling voice: "Minerva, this is Remica at the Big Apple Bakery! Are you alone?"

The doctor eyed Otto, pressed a finger to her lips. "Just me and my patients."

"Well, lock up and stay inside. There's trouble at Town Square. That strange woman from the mirror emporium is there with that ghastly brute of a man."

The Judge! Otto thought.

Dr. Medina's fur bristled. "No. Not again."

"Lenny from Lopsided Furniture Company said the sheriff wouldn't stand by anymore. He confronted him, and"—Miss Remica sniffled—"you know."

Otto was pretty sure the town's sheriff was cooling his

heels in a mirror cell. Along with anyone else who dared challenge the Judge.

"Well," Dr. Medina said, "it's about time someone stood up for Fry. I refuse to cower in my own town anymore. I'm going to Town Square to stand with anyone else brave enough to resist this nonsense."

"You're insane, Minerva."

"It's more insane to do nothing. If no one opposes them, they'll never stop."

"I'll be in my store baking. If you survive, you're welcome to some fresh apple fritters."

"Your support is ever so comforting. Goodbye."

There was an audible *CLICK* as the line went dead.

Otto began to speak, but Dr. Medina held up a finger again and whispered, "Let me hang up the phone first."

She crossed the room, gathered the boxy phone she'd tossed a moment ago, returned to the frayed wires on the wall, and hung the phone back on its mount. "Come on. We're going to see what all this rigamarole is about."

Otto said, "Are you sure that's smart?"

Dr. Medina quickly rechecked all the animal cages, with Otto closely tailing her. "Smart, I'm not sure. Necessary, absolutely."

Her final stop was at the wolverine's cage. She sniffed it, then Otto, and said, "I'm glad you relaxed a bit. I distinctly remember the scent of fear when you first laid eyes on this sweet animal."

"We're cool." Otto hoped whatever scent he emitted didn't somehow reveal the truth.

Otto wasn't afraid because he'd already learned this wolverine was way more mellow than the one back home. While Dr. Medina was grabbing supplies from her closet, Otto tiptoed by its cage, opened the medicine cabinet, and snatched a vial of Fixityall, now concealed in his cargo pants pocket.

The whole time, the once terrifying creature never made a sound.

17

Finding Yourself

SHEED MADE IT TO GRANDMA'S HOUSE without any trouble, finding it largely recognizable. And unexpectedly large.

It was still the color of sunshine. Still had a garden around the side and a swing on the porch. The differences came in the scale. It was approximately triple the size of the version he and Otto lived in. More like Grandma's mansion.

Because it was so big, he felt most comfortable observing it from a distance, to get a grip on what other sort of Warped World effects may have altered this familiar space. Or—more importantly—altered this world's Otto, Sheed, and Grandma. Whatever surprises he encountered, and he was sure there'd be some, he wanted a moment to adjust before diving in.

He perched halfway up the slope of Harkness Hill to

watch from high ground. Just as he got there, someone emerged from the house. Grandma.

Sheed's heart warmed at the sight of her. From what he could tell, she was the same as his world's Grandma. She had on a blue church dress and a big ole church hat with a brim the width of a UFO, a Bible tucked under her arm, and what looked like a baking pan of biscuits in her hand.

She stepped on the porch, closing the screen door gently behind her, then yelled, "Boys, I'm leaving for choir rehearsal now. Y'all be good."

Sheed couldn't pick up the voices on the inside, but he imagined some version of him and Otto yelling back, "Okay, Grandma!"

Grandma descended the porch steps . . . and paused.

Sheed checked the gravel driveway that stretched from the main road. Checked to the right of the house, and the left. He didn't see Grandma's car, and she didn't seem to be looking for it either.

She was looking up.

Wings—white, fluffy—unfurled from the brim of Grandma's church hat. They gave one mighty flap, separating Grandma's feet from the ground. Two more flaps, and she'd cleared the roof. Grandma continued rising, higher and higher, the wings from her hat spread wide, eventually catching a tailwind and drifting toward her church on the north side of Fry.

Sheed stared after his flying grandma for a long time,

his attention drawn back to the house only when the screen door slammed.

There were two men on the porch. One ridiculously tall and skinny. The other, a more reasonable height, and familiar in a way Sheed wasn't prepared for, though he thought he'd gotten used to Warped World strangeness. He squinted and whispered, "TimeStar?"

Sheed was a little too far away to see his face clearly, but the height and build and dreadlocks were reminiscent of the time traveling hero who'd come from the future to help them fight Mr. Flux on the last day of summer.

How was he back?

How was he *here?*

He must've known they were in trouble, Sheed reasoned. He maybe had a device that could help!

Sheed ran down Harkness Hill, waving his arms and shouting, "TimeStar! TimeStar!"

The two men faced him as he crossed the last dozen yards to the porch. He skidded to a stop in the dewy grass, recognizing these weren't men at all. They were big like men, but they had smooth baby faces. Faces he knew.

It's me. Us! Otto and Sheed. Warped Worlded.

"Can we help you?" Warped World Sheed asked, a normal kid's voice squeaking from his stretched, lanky frame.

Do I really sound like that? Sheed thought, too stupefied to respond.

Warped World Otto said, "Are you in some kind of

trouble? We can help. We're legends around these parts. The premier heroes of Logan—"

"Chill, Otto." Warped World Sheed crouched so they were eye to eye. "He's obviously confused about something. Hey, little person, did you hit your head?"

Still no words. There were thoughts! Lots of thoughts.

Sheed coming face-to-face with himself didn't feel strange at all. Warped World Sheed was tall like a basketball player. The height needed to jump over a bunch of defenders for a super highlight dunk. He was handsome. Not *more* handsome, thank you very much, Mad Scientist Leen.

Sheed's gaze kept floating to the one who'd introduced

himself as Otto. It was Otto's voice, all right. Otto's legendary ego, for sure. The dreadlocks were shorter, and there was no beard because this was still a kid, even if he was a little bigger. So why'd he look so much like a young TimeStar?

"What's your name?" TimeStar Otto asked.

Sheed knew in his gut this was not the time for the absolute truth. There was too much uncertainty swirling around his head. Along with something scary floating at the edge of his thoughts.

"I'm, ummm"—he glanced to Grandma's shrubs— "*Bush . . . ler.*"

TimeStar Otto's face scrunched. "Your name is Bushler?"

"Yeah." Sheed's usual annoyance toward Otto spiked. "You got a problem with that? Can I live, bruh?"

Warped World Sheed chuckled, while Warped World Otto scowled at the sudden attitude.

Bushler Sheed did not chuckle or scowl. He shuddered. His own words replayed in his head. *Can I live?*

That scary thing on the edge of his brain was still fuzzy, still slightly out of reach. Yet . . .

Why did this version of Otto look . . . like . . . TimeStar?

A shrill ringing interrupted introductions. TimeStar Otto fished a small device from his pocket, something like a cell phone. If it was a cell phone, then this world's Grandma was way different, because the one back home told Otto and Sheed they couldn't have phones until they were, like, thirty.

TimeStar Otto glanced at the display in his palm, then whipped his head to Warped World Sheed. "It's the Legend Alert. Mayor Ahmed says something's going down in Town Square."

"You guys have a Legend Alert?" Sheed wished he carried a notepad like his cousin, because he'd definitely write that down. The coolness of an alert system vanished as that nagging thought slammed into his head again.

Why does he look like TimeStar?

Warped World Sheed said, "We should grab the bikes and get to town quick." He cocked a thumb toward Bushler Sheed. "What about him?"

"Bushler can come along," TimeStar Otto said, "That's what the handlebars are for."

Sheed had heard his Otto say that same thing a hundred times. It had never felt creepy before.

The creepiest part was yet to come.

From his seat on TimeStar Otto's handlebars, Sheed saw an excessive number of potholes in the road ahead. The boys weaved their bikes around them, and as they passed, Sheed noticed these were actually pots *and* holes. A variety of pots—cast iron, sterling silver, Teflon—were littered about. Between them, there were holes. Black openings the size of wagon wheels that sucked air and light into the asphalt. Sheed leaned to stare into a hole they passed a little too closely for comfort. There was no bottom that he could see. He did not look into a hole again.

"Do you know what's happening in Town Square?" Sheed asked.

TimeStar Otto said, "No. Mayor Ahmed usually tells us when we get there."

That sounded about right. Sheed had an inkling that this had something to do with Missus Nedraw and the Judge's search for Nevan and his "gang." He nearly began discussing theories as if he was talking to his Otto, then remembered he was Bushler, at least for the time being, and it was best not to reveal too much knowledge until he understood this all better.

Sheed said, "When did you start growing dreadlocks?"

"I didn't grow them. First day of school I woke up, and they were there. You know how it goes."

Sheed was starting to understand. Sort of. Things just happened in Warped World. Like the park turning into a grassy tidal wave, and his Otto's arm turning to stone. So not like his world, though there were connections that couldn't be pure coincidence.

TimeStar Otto's dreadlocks appeared when he woke up for the first day of school? So the day *after* the last day of summer.

The day *after* they defeated Mr. Flux and changed time.

The day *after* a dreadlock-wearing TimeStar went back to the future.

In Sheed's world.

But did all that happen here, too? "Was something going on the day before that? Did you get a Legend Alert?"

"Naw. The last day of summer was boring." TimeStar Otto jerked his head toward Warped World Sheed. "I tried to get him to go on one last adventure, but he wanted to sleep all day."

"Yep. Sure did," Warped World Sheed said.

No Mr. Flux, then. No frozen time. No Clock Watchers.

Yet this Otto looked freakily similar to the guy who showed up out of nowhere that day. Or . . . was it the other way around?

Did Otto look like TimeStar, or did TimeStar look like Otto? What did that difference mean? *Was* there a difference?

They'd cleared the pots and holes, and coasted by the WELCOME TO FRY, VIRGINIA sign. Though Town Square was just a short ride away, TimeStar Otto squeezed his hand brake and brought them to stop just inside the city limits.

"What you doing?" Sheed said.

"We gotta go do Legend Stuff," said TimeStar Otto. "Wouldn't want you to get hurt."

"Get hurt?" Sheed sneered. "But I'm a—"

No. He wasn't a legend, too. Not to these guys.

They were at the curb just before the turn onto Main Street, which led directly to Town Square. Sheed could find his own way if need be. What he really wanted to find was his Otto and ask him some very pointed questions. So he hopped off the handlebars and gave TimeStar Otto and Warped World Sheed a fist bump each. "Be careful, guys."

Warped World Sheed said, "Where's the fun in that?"

They sailed away on their bikes, leaving Sheed to walk and wonder.

He drifted toward Town Square slowly, more than willing to let the local legends handle whatever danger might be present. If he knew his cousin—and recent developments made him doubt if he actually did know his cousin, but still—Sheed was willing to bet Otto would be heading there, too.

Dr. Medina led the way. At the intersection where several of the strangely curved Fry roads opened up on to the expansive Town Square, a loose crowd had formed to watch the commotion at the bandstand just east of the founder's statue.

Back home the raised platform supported various bands that came to Fry throughout the year. Rock-and-roll. Country Western. Rap. R&B. The Fry community loved all kinds of sounds and good times. That's not what this was.

Where a drum kit might usually sit, there was a big-time mirror. Where backup singers normally stood was the Judge, his leather book splayed wide in one hand while he held his giant gavel upright with the other. At the head of the stage, in the lead singer's position, was Mayor Ahmed

—who looked pretty similar to the version Otto was used to in his gray suit and bright orange tie. Except he was crying, and on his knees, and apparently begging the Judge for mercy.

Unlike the concerts Otto was used to, and would've preferred, there were no microphones here; he couldn't hear what was being said on the stage—the crowd was just too loud. Dr. Medina wedged her way through, and Otto continued in her wake. The closer they got, the more he could make out one side of the conversation because of the Judge's booming voice.

". . . the Law is very clear on this matter. Your town is harboring fugitives. This cannot go unpunished."

Dr. Medina had gotten them very close, so Otto heard Mayor Ahmed's response, sounding as reasonable as he always did in the face of the unique and fantastic dangers that tended to fall upon Fry. "Nooooo! No more, sir! We don't want the kinds of problems you're bringing. We're simple people."

The mayor wept.

The Judge said, "Someone here knows something. That someone will speak."

He clapped the butt of his gavel on the stage, and the mallet head glowed with purple energy. From the crowd, a plump man became encased in the same energy that pulsed from the gavel, yelping as he levitated into the air like a helium balloon. "Hey, hey, hey!"

The plump man was drawn to the stage, where he hovered between the Judge and the mayor, his squirming bulk reflected in the mirror there.

Mayor Ahmed spoke through sobs. "Oh, leave Herm alone. He doesn't know anything."

The Judge decided he wanted to hear directly from Herm. "Where can I find Nevan the Nightmare and his gang?"

Herm said, "I don't know who the heck that is, Mister."

The Judge glanced at the pages of his book, then back to Herm. "False witness!"

With another slight motion from the gavel, Herm was flung into the mirror.

The crowd gasped, and in the brief moment Herm passed through the magical glass, causing it to ripple like water, Otto made out a dozen trapped, silently screaming faces already imprisoned within.

The surface became solid glass again.

"That's quite enough!" Dr. Medina shouted, pushing even closer to the stage.

Otto considered following — probably would've — if a hand hadn't clamped onto his stony arm like a vise, dragging him in the opposite direction.

Missus Nedraw had snuck up on him, grabbed him, and was dragging him away from the action. "Stop! What are you doing?" said Otto.

She kept tugging, mumbling, "Out of the way" and

"Excuse me," and trampling over townsfolk too slow to recognize the danger they were in.

They'd cleared the crowd and were about to make the turn toward the emporium when Otto undid the zipper on his coat, slipping out of it — and Missus Nedraw's grip — and skidding to a halt on the sidewalk.

She walked another few feet dragging the discarded coat before realizing what he'd done. She said, "Are you crazy? We need to get you home, pronto."

"You brought me here!" Otto countered.

"Brought *us* here!" Sheed rounded the corner, having clocked the commotion of Missus Nedraw snatching Otto up.

Otto's face twitched when he saw Sheed, partially from happiness, mostly from knowing he had a lot of explaining to do. Still, he embraced his cousin. "Sheed! You're okay."

Sheed did not hug back. "You mean after you left me in an underground cave with giant spiders?"

"What underground cave?" Missus Nedraw asked. "And what happened to your arms, Octavius?"

She came closer and poked the rocky skin with her index finger.

Otto's stone arms protruded sharp and gray from his shirt. Funny how he'd almost gotten used to it. Though he wasn't used to the creeping cold sensation itching along his stomach and toward his feet. The change was spreading faster.

Missus Nedraw shook her head dismissively. "No worries, as soon as you cross back into your world, the change should reverse."

She attempted to grab him again, but Otto dodged. "No. Not yet."

Misdirections and half truths shifted in his head as he prepared to explain his reluctance to return home without revealing that Sheed needed to take the medicine in Otto's pocket before they left Warped World. Despite Dr. Medina's warning.

How bad could the side effects really be?

Sheed said, "Otto's right. We can't leave yet."

That . . . was totally unexpected. "Yeah! I'm right," Otto said, rolling with it. "Though, why do *you* think I'm right?"

"Because we, er, *us*, er, *this world's versions of us* are about to get into a fight, I think."

Missus Nedraw's face went slack. "Someone here is going to challenge the Judge?"

"Challenge and win," Sheed said. "That's what we, er, they, do."

"No, no, no, no, no," Missus Nedraw stammered. "That is a very bad idea."

Otto's heart raced. "It's not just them. Dr. Medina, too. You dragged me away, and she needed my help."

But Missus Nedraw seemed to know what the boys had yet to understand. It was way too late to help.

An anguished howl sounded from the stage. Over the

crowd Otto saw Dr. Medina, floating, encased in a shell of purple energy just before being tossed into the Judge's mirror like Herm and the other poor Fry residents.

Otto nearly shrieked, but was stunned silent when two more individuals hopped on stage to confront the Judge.

"You know those guys?" Sheed asked Otto, his voice a low grumble. "Do they look familiar?"

Otto knew who they were, though their looks weren't anything he ever would've expected. The tall, lanky one in athletic wear was Sheed, obviously. The other one made his heart flutter. This world's version of Otto looked way too much like TimeStar for comfort. He wasn't an adult, and he didn't have a beard, and his dreadlocks weren't quite as long, but the look was the look.

All of a sudden, Otto's entire torso, plus his calves, began to itch . . . the rocky skin leaping to previously unaffected portions of his body.

It was nowhere near as uncomfortable as Sheed's narrow-eyed stare.

TimeStar Otto spoke to Warped World Sheed, then dropped into a crouch. Warped World Sheed sprinted toward him, then leapt, planting one foot on his Otto's shoulders before springing toward the Judge.

Maneuver #65 — the trampoline.

It's supposed to go like this: Sheed flings himself at the target, pulling a concealed net from his shirt. While he's in the air, Otto tosses a homemade bola—a length of rope with a weighted ball on each end—at the target's ankles. While the bola wraps and binds the target's legs, the net snags his upper body. In a perfect world, this ends the target's reign of terror.

Warped World is far from perfect.

The Judge, though big, was quick. He dropped the Law into the holster on his hip and jerked forward as Warped World Sheed went airborne, ducking under the flying boy and closing the gap between him and the blubbering Mayor Ahmed. TimeStar Otto's bola whirled toward the Judge, but the giant simply snatched Mayor Ahmed into its path so the rope coiled around the Fry leader. The Judge remained free and cranky. He frowned deeply beneath his dark, oily hair.

"Assaulting a judge is against the law!" he boomed, loud enough for regular Otto and Sheed to hear him, even from the back of the crowd.

The Judge activated his gavel, the purple energy crackling as it encased Warped World Sheed and TimeStar Otto. The boys did not have time to scream as they were tossed into that mirror.

Though their counterparts did.

Regular Otto and Sheed cried out, horrified to see versions of themselves trapped so . . . *easily*. And for how long? A hundred years? A thousand? Forever?

Because the crowd had grown silent, lest the Judge notice them, too, the boys' screams carried. The Judge turned their way, pointing his gavel in their direction. "You."

The Judge leapt from the stage, shoved his way through the crowd.

Missus Nedraw hopped between him and the boys. Faced them. "Run to the emporium as fast as you can. Right now."

She did not need to tell them twice.

18

The Perils of Not Changing the Locks

OTTO THOUGHT HE'D SLOW THEM DOWN, given his extra, rocky weight. But he moved swiftly. Now that the stony hardness and strength had spread to his legs, he found his extra bulk easy to manage. Warped World had some benefits.

Sheed was not as quick as usual. He coughed as he ran. Coughed and could not stop. Grandma would've said he'd "swallowed wrong," then patted him on the back, but since she wasn't there, he was forced to jog and gasp.

Missus Nedraw drew up close behind him, planting a hand on Sheed's back and nudging him forward. "You're going to want to hurry up, dear."

Sheed focused on Otto, imagined his cousin as a moving finish line. With his chest burning and tears in his eyes, he pushed on. He felt terrible all of a sudden and didn't know why.

The Main Street businesses were a blur on either side of them. The gyrations and shifts of the architecture seemed more frantic than before. It was almost as if the buildings were shivering with fright. As Sheed glanced over his shoulder, he couldn't say he blamed them.

Several dozen yards behind them, but gaining, was the Judge, sprinting like a track star mixed with a gorilla. The Law bounced on his hip, and he gripped his gavel tightly. His robe flapped mightily with his speed, and each footfall cracked the asphalt, sending newly loosed pebbles flying.

Sheed decided it was best not to focus on him and looked to Otto, who'd stretched the gap between them even further. *When did I get so slow?* Sheed thought.

They were approaching the emporium. Otto veered toward the door, his stony hand outstretched. He was moving too fast and couldn't quite stop in time. He braced for impact.

But when Otto's hand touched the wood, the door swung open easily on a well-oiled hinge.

Sheed crossed the threshold a few moments later, along with Missus Nedraw. She slammed the door behind them and engaged the lock.

"Will that keep him out?" Otto asked.

Missus Nedraw, slow in answering, stared at the deadbolt. "It should've kept us out." Concern crinkled her brow. "Who unlocked this door?"

From the depths of the emporium hopped Nevan,

cloaked in shadow, a golden key ring pinched between his long, veiny fingers. When he spoke, his voice was significantly deeper than before. "That would be me, Evie. It seems my key still works."

Missus Nedraw dropped into a fighting stance, a useless effort. Two spiders attacked at once, bounding from either side of the door. The one on Missus Nedraw's left shoved her with six arms. The one on the right held a full-length mirror at the ready. Missus Nedraw flew through the glass into one of the very cells she'd once been responsible for. The glass rippled, then solidified with a sound like bars slamming into place.

From the other side of the glass, Miss Nedraw flung herself forward, rebounding off the surface, yelling things Otto and Sheed could not hear.

Their natural instinct was to help, but before they could lunge to break the glass, webs snagged their arms and legs, suspending them inches off the ground. More spiders descended from the ceiling.

Spencer hung upside down, face-to-face with Otto. "Sorry there, mate. Nevan says we gotta ask you some questions, and it's best you can't move when we do."

"Before that, one more bit of business," Nevan said from behind him. Sheed strained his neck, attempting to look over his shoulder, but could only see a silhouette. A large silhouette.

"In front of the door," Nevan said. "Now!"

Two of the Jurors were holding an extremely tall, extremely wide mirror, one on either side of the frame. They positioned it before the emporium's front door, the glass facing the street.

The stampeding, determined Judge burst into the emporium and ran right into the extra-large mirror.

He did it with such force, the mirror lurched in the Jurors' hands, nearly causing a fumble.

"Hold on!" Nevan barked.

The only thing that didn't go through was the Judge's giant book of laws, which got caught on the mirror's frame, popping loose from its holster and sliding across the floor. A spider snatched it up with a web and hurled it to Nevan, who tucked it under his arm.

The Jurors recovered quickly, rotating the mirror for all to see. On the other side of the glass, the furious Judge pounded with fists and his gavel. Though the mirror frame jumped and gyrated from the blows, the glass did not give.

"My disobedient Executioner," Nevan said, "seeing you in there, at my mercy, is as satisfying as I anticipated. How is it seeing me in my preferred form, old friend?"

The creature, who'd once been tiny, maybe a little cute, stepped from the shadows. The boys gasped.

Otto, who knew a little something about the physical fluctuations possible in Warped World, still found what he was seeing hard to believe. His heart thundered in his rocky chest.

Nevan, the tiny kangaroo thing they'd met a few hours ago, was over eight feet tall, with muscles that bulged beneath his stretched and strained robe like water balloons. He looked like he weighed five hundred pounds and could bench-press a bus. Yet his head was still as tiny as before. Which made his entire stunning transformation that much freakier.

He turned his itty-bitty head to the boys. "Now, what to do with you?"

Neither Otto nor Sheed was sure he wanted to know the answer to *that* question.

19

The Chapter Where the Villain Tells You His Plan

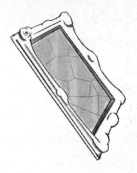

NEVAN HAD THE JURORS and the spiders arrange Missus Nedraw's mirror, the Judge's mirror, and web-stuck Otto and Sheed in a row. Then he hopped over, tiny head bobbing and thick body-builder arms crossing his barrel chest. After a dozen passes or so, he stopped before Otto and Sheed, and said, "You two are children. It's quite possible that Evie Nedraw and my former Executioner corrupted you with lies. Doesn't seem quite right to punish you for being deceived."

The boys said nothing, because they weren't sure they'd been deceived. Perhaps the Judge, or Executioner, or whatever he was, wasn't the greatest guy, but Nevan's behavior left something to be desired, too.

Sheed said, "Can you get us out of these webs, then talk about it? My arms are hurting."

Otto felt a painful twinge in his gut when he thought

about Sheed suffering in their uncomfortable, suspended position. It was the only pain he felt.

His rocky arms didn't hurt. At all. He'd been in the same awkward position as Sheed for the same amount of time, yet he felt fine. Not just fine. He felt strong.

Otto wondered . . .

Subtly, careful not to draw Nevan's attention, he tugged at his web-bonds, felt some give.

Nevan told Sheed, "Whether or not I can release you depends. You see, I have a proposition. I've seen you two in action. You're smart, know the right things to say. You were able to fool my less discerning spider friends into believing you were on the right side of our particular conflict.

That . . . is valuable. More valuable than locking two kids away in a mirror for all of time."

The big-mouth hippo-looking Juror said, "Mostly because we haven't figured out the financials of kid-size mirrors."

Nevan stared daggers. "Harvey—"

The hippo kept going, seemingly thinking out loud. "We could probably make smaller, cheaper mirrors, but still charge the same price as big mirrors for a better profit margin."

"HARVEY!"

The Juror snapped out of his motor-mouth daze. "Yeah, boss?"

"When I talk, you don't. Got it?"

Harvey huffed, but remained quiet.

"As I was saying," Nevan continued. "Ever since we were locked away eight—" Nevan stopped abruptly, his eyes darting between the boys and the spiders. Then he cupped a huge fist to his tiny mouth and made a show of coughing.

He said something he didn't mean to say, Otto thought, attempting to replay the words in his head, so he might record it in his Legendary Log later. Though his attention was divided between the muscular monologuing kangaroo and the slowly slackening web anchoring him in place.

Spencer asked Nevan, "You all right there, friend?"

"Just a little dust in my throat. Ever since we got locked

away *a long time ago*, we've become unfamiliar with current customs in the various worlds our mirrors currently service or might service in the future. Having a pair of bright young emissaries like yourselves could help the spread of righteous justice."

"Hold up!" said Sheed. "You want us to help you take mirror emporiums into more worlds so you can keep getting rich locking people up for dumb stuff?"

Nevan grinned. "To be clear, you could get very rich, too. That is one of your options. Then there's the other."

Nevan motioned to a quartet of Jurors, who scampered off into the emporium shadows. They returned with a pair of mirrors on rolling carts. Cells. For the boys.

Nevan, almost compassionate with his request, said, "I'm going to need an answer, boys. Are you with me or against me?"

Sheed wondered if those mirror cells were cramped. Figured he'd find out soon enough.

Then Otto spoke for them. "We're going to need a little more time to think about it."

Something snapped with a *Twang!* Otto had torn the web holding his right arm. He did the same with his left. Quicker than quick, he yanked his legs free.

Nevan roared, "No! Get them."

Otto leapt, chopping through the webs holding Sheed's hands, then looped an arm around his waist, tugging him free of the webs binding his legs. He was stronger and faster than he'd ever been. Strong and fast enough to escape Nevan's trap. For the moment.

Nevan and his followers blocked the main entrance, so Otto ran with a destination in mind much farther than any they could reach by simply going through the front door. Deeper into the emporium they went.

"What are you doing?" Sheed yelled, bouncing on Otto's hip, "Where are we going?"

"I'm thinking."

Many footfalls pattered behind them. Nevan shouting orders to bring the boys back, to throw them in their cells immediately.

Otto passed the Bathroom Mirror Mass Communication System aisle, then the short-range-travel mirror aisle, then made a skidding turn onto the aisle of mirrors that led to all sorts of other worlds, including their own. That would've been his preferred destination, except the aisle was long, seeming to stretch into infinity. And Nevan's people were gaining.

As Otto raced past mirrors, he threw quick glances right and left, trying to judge the nature of a particular mirror's destination by its unique frame. The deep space cosmos frame seemed like a bad idea. The molten lava frame seemed even worse. He slowed at the sight of a frame that had colorful gummi bears carved in the top and really large teeth carved in the bottom, and didn't quite know what to make of that one, so he kept it moving.

The spiders had gone high, swinging for increased speed, and would be on them at any second. Slung webs splattered the ground near Otto's feet, near misses. He had to make a choice. Fast!

He kept running, kept passing the strange and confusing frames. He even managed an additional burst of speed past the darkly veiled Black Mirror that would show you what you look like on the day before you die.

Then he saw a familiar frame coming up fast on the right, one he'd noticed on their side of the mirror before traveling to Warped World.

It was coral colored, overlapping pink and beige. When Otto first saw it, he thought he heard the ocean, and since it was either go or be captured, he said a silent prayer: *Please let this be a beach world. Please let this be a beach world.*

Right before a spider leg could clamp down on his shoulder, he flung himself and Sheed at the mirror's surface, and broke through into another world.

Sadly, it was not a beach.

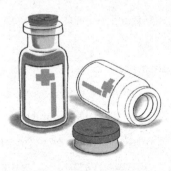

SHEED WOULD NEVER GET USED TO that crazy sensation of traveling but not traveling. It was the best way he could describe pushing through the mirror's surface into another world, but crashing onto the emporium floor in a way that felt like you hadn't gone anywhere at all. Except, there were some differences here. Extreme ones. Starting with the puddle he found himself in.

Otto had lost his grip, so Sheed was no longer suspended on his cousin's hip. Instead he lay face-down before the Warped World funhouse mirror in a large patch of stagnant water that reminded him of storm drains and sewers.

"Ewwww!" Pushing himself off the ground, convinced his coat would be ruined by the muck, Sheed prepared to be grossed out even more. Not so. He wasn't wearing the coat he'd had on all day.

What now covered his top half was the same red as his

coat. What covered his bottom half was the same blue as his jeans. This new outfit wasn't either of those things, but a skintight one-piece wetsuit, like what surfers wear.

Otto was sprawled a few feet away in another damp spot, also in a wetsuit that matched the colors of the clothes he'd left Grandma's house in. He wasn't part stone anymore, either. Regular Otto skin, in a regular Otto shape, though both of them looked ready for a scuba diving lesson, which made Sheed uncomfortable. Discomfort turned to panic when he examined the Warped World mirror, anticipating anywhere from two to eight arms to poke through and snatch them back.

"Otto, get up. They might be coming after us."

Otto, shaken but scurrying, got to his feet, knees bent for sprinting. He did a quick self-assessment — stone gone, wearing a wetsuit, huh? — but focused mainly on Sheed's very probable concern.

When seconds passed and nobody from Warped World followed them here, new concerns bubbled in Otto's mind. *Why* hadn't anyone come after them?

The boys stared at the mirror, only their own distorted awkward reflections staring back. Then a familiar, unsettling sound warbled through the glass. The sound of a lock clanking into place.

The boys looked at each other, then Sheed made the risky maneuver of reaching toward the glass, through it, or trying to. His palm pressed flat against the mirror's surface as if it was, indeed, a normal mirror. There was no give, no pushing through into Warped World.

Sheed whispered, "They locked us out."

If it was a mirror that was also a door, then it made sense that it could be locked. Otto couldn't shake the sinking feeling that there was more to this, though. Something they were missing. First Nevan didn't send his cronies after them. Then he locked them in this very damp version of the emporium.

Otto said, "Let's go see where we are."

They made the long walk to the end of the aisle. Turning the corner, they found an oblong digital clock mounted to the shelf's endcap. It read 01:25:43.

Otto spared it but a glance. The time of day wasn't all that important right now.

Heading toward the general direction of the emporium's front end, they looked for the exit. Eventually they cleared the shelves and found it. Though they didn't get closer than a dozen yards to the emporium doors. The huge display windows on either side told them all they needed to know.

Beyond the glass, Fry citizens moved along main street with shopping bags, eyes on their phones, doing other generally normal, generally carefree, Saturday afternoon things. That they all were fish swimming the depths of a murky blue underwater version of Fry . . . was a little upsetting.

"Otto," Sheed said, barely a whisper, "we're in Wet World."

. . .

Sheed quickened his pace, no longer concerned with the cleanliness of the puddles he splashed through. His path had taken him closer to the windows than Otto liked. Sheed pressed his face to the glass like someone trying to get up close and personal with sharks at an aquarium, peered up. After that, he looked even more distraught. "I don't see the surface. How deep are we?"

Very, Otto had already concluded.

While Sheed paced, trying to take it all in, Otto sat, writing slow, contemplative notes.

ENTRY #67

I am confident that this mirror was a better choice than the one with the frame made of buzz saws. Or the one rimmed in tiger's teeth. How much better? Unclear. The fact that Nevan and crow chose to lock us out of Warped World instead of pursue us here is both a relief and troubling. We have some time to think. But . . . were they worried about us or this place?

DEDUCTION: Stay alert.

Otto said, "How weird is it that they didn't come after us?"

"Not the weirdest thing I've seen today."

That was Sheed's cranky voice. The shock of the trip was wearing off. They weren't in immediate danger. There was no maneuver to get Otto out of this.

He hopped up from his cross-legged position on the damp floor, craned his neck, spun in a circle, hoping for a change of subject. "We have to figure our next move. Maybe there's something in this emporium we can use to—"

"Why did you look like TimeStar, Otto?" Sheed's back was to the window. A creature that looked something like a stingray, but with long blond hair and a purse, swam by behind him.

Otto forced a laugh. "Me? Look like TimeStar? No way."

"Not *you* you. The other you. The one who went onstage with the other me and got locked in a mirror cell by the Judge. I know you saw it."

"Pffft. Did I?" Otto made wide eyes. "Hello. I might need glasses."

"Stop it, Otto." Sheed didn't yell. It was a quiet command, almost too low to hear over the drips and dribbles of water that were constant background noise in this overly moist version of the emporium. That shook Otto. A yelling Sheed was a Sheed he was used to.

"The TimeStar we met on the last day of summer."

Sheed moved away from window, crossing shadows as he drew near Otto. "Was he you? From the future?"

"Sheed, I—I mean, him—it's—" Otto's tongue wouldn't work right. His brain didn't know correct words. He felt panicked enough to dive through the display window and swim for it. He clamped his mouth shut.

Sheed, close enough to touch, simply stared. Waiting for his answer.

Otto sniffed, his eyes burning, until two tears were needed to douse the guilty fire in him. He whispered, "Yes. He was me."

"So where was I? I mean, future me?" Sheed's soft voice quaked.

Otto couldn't answer that question. Not with words. His sobs took every bit of air, and energy, and love that he had. He hugged himself against the pain of having the horrible truth of Sheed's future torn from him.

Sheed's 'fro and shoulders slumped. "That's what I thought."

Then he made a joke, the kind they'd learned at school is called "gallows humor," because you tell it in a desperate situation and it's not really so funny. "This time I wish you *were* the only one good at deductions."

21

A Name and Desire

SUDDENLY THE BIG PROBLEM OF BEING STUCK in the mirror emporium underwater, in another dimension, felt like a small problem. One barely worth Sheed's time. If he had much time left at all. "How does it happen? I mean, what goes wrong? Is it soon?"

Otto sniveled, scrubbed away tears with the meaty part of his hand. He opened his mouth like he might answer. No words came.

Some small voice inside Sheed, sounding a little bit like Grandma, said, *Hug him!* He took a step forward to do it.

Until a larger voice in his head, his own, reminded him, *Otto knew and didn't say anything.* That made Sheed mad. He liked feeling mad over feeling whatever it was that had his stomach twisting and made him scared to take even a single step in any direction because what if that step was his last?

The Grandma voice returned and whispered, *Maybe that's the reason Otto didn't tell you.*

Sheed stopped listening to the Grandma voice and yelled at his cousin. "That's why you kept bringing up doctors all the time. That's why you kept looking at me weird when you thought I didn't notice. You . . . you . . . you're *sooooo wack*, Otto!"

Otto lurched backwards, as if Sheed had hit him harder than any punch in the history of Legendary Alston Boy punches. His tears ceased, and his face went slack. For them, being called wack was the coldest insult. Fighting words.

"I. Am. Not," Otto stated emphatically.

"Are too! Wack. Wack. Wack," Sheed said, not just feeling mad now. Feeling mean.

"Am. Not!" Although crossing into Wet World had converted their clothing to wetsuits, Otto's pockets still bulged with all the things he carried. He dug in, fished out the slingshot he'd taken from the Warped World armory. In his rage he tossed the whole slingshot at Sheed—it wasn't what he'd intended to show his stupid cousin.

The weapon bounced off Sheed's chest before he caught it two-handed, looking wholly confused.

Otto dug in his other pocket, grabbing what he'd meant to show Sheed, the vial of miracle medicine he'd taken from Dr. Medina's office. "I didn't bother telling you the bad news because I was planning to save your life with this!"

He thrust the vial of bright yellow liquid at Sheed. The ultimate see-I-told-you-so.

Only the vial wasn't filled with glowing miracle cure.

The liquid in it was clear.

"What's that supposed to be?" Sheed asked.

Otto . . . wasn't . . . sure. His gut told him it wasn't medicine, not anymore. He pocketed the vial and went for his notepad.

ENTRY #68

We came here and our clothes changed to suitable Wet World attire. Did the trip change the Fixityall, too? Is it now just water, no different from the kind pressing against the emporium windows?

DEDUCTION: Maybe

Sheed yanked the pad from Otto's hand. "Are you writing about me? Do you have a bunch of notes on my condition? You could write it in your little pads but couldn't tell me?"

Otto rushed forward, swiping for his pad. "Give it back!"

Sheed, taller and faster, backpedaled, water splashing at his feet while holding the pad high and out of reach.

"That stuff in your pocket looked like Grandma's insulin," Sheed said. "Do I have problems with my sugar like her?"

"No. This isn't insulin. You don't have her diabetes. I don't think."

"You don't *think*."

Otto couldn't argue and work on this problem in his head. Also, he was feeling a little mean now, too. "Shut up and let me solve this, you idiot."

Sheed's face went from creased with anger to smooth and emotionless.

"Tell me how you really feel, Otto, biggest brain of them all."

Otto knew, as far as they were from their version of Logan, Fry, and Grandma's house, that in that moment and that moment only, he'd taken things a bit too far.

"Sheed, I'm sorry. I shouldn't have said that."

"When's what you should and shouldn't do ever stopped you before?" Sheed dropped Otto's pad in a puddle and stomped off into the depths of the emporium.

"Sheed, I'm really sorry," Otto shouted after him. "You can punch me if you want."

Sheed didn't even look back.

Otto fished his pad from the ankle-deep water. Figuring it was probably ruined but unable to toss it, he stuck it back in his wetsuit pocket, then paced along the front of the emporium, thinking it best to let Sheed cool off.

Walking by the display windows, he kept a cautious distance from the glass that separated him from the murky blue water beyond. Finding the sight of passing fish people too unsettling, he changed direction and moved toward the checkout counter. He noticed movement beneath the cash register. Curious, he stepped behind the counter into that typically forbidden area of most shops that is reserved for Employees Only.

The movement that caught his eye was a digital clock similar to the one he'd spotted when they first arrived a little over an hour ago: 00:22:02.

Then . . .

00:22:01

00:22:00

00:21:59

Not a clock, then. A timer. Counting down.

To what?

Concern and logic broke through Otto's sense that Sheed needed alone time. Despite his reluctance, he felt quite strongly that maybe he should go get his cousin. Right now.

"Sheed!"

Otto went on the run. Occasionally droplets pattered his face like light rain, as if the roof were leaking. Rows and rows of mirrors passed by in a blur. Otto peeked down each row he passed but feared he already knew exactly where to find Sheed.

On the improbably long row of mirror portals to other worlds, he spotted Sheed in the distance.

He was standing before the veiled Black Mirror. The mirror that showed anyone who dared peer into it what they would look like on the last full day of their life.

Otto's heart fell into his shoes. "Sheed, don't!"

Sheed glared at him, still mad. He took a defiant step toward the covered mirror.

Otto sprinted then. But he was still too slow and too far away to prevent Sheed from grabbing the veil covering the mirror and yanking it away. It drifted lightly, like a leaf on the wind, but Otto swore he heard it hit the ground, a sound like an axe falling.

Otto came to a stop a few yards short of his cousin, who stared into the dark glass with no emotion whatsoever on his face. What did he see? *When* did he see?

The Black Mirror was not what Sheed expected. It didn't show an actual reflection. None of the shelves, or other strange mirrors behind him, were visible. It showed no parts of his surroundings at all. Only him, as he would be at the end of his life, and nothing else.

"Sheed?" said Otto. He stood at an angle, unable to see what the glass showed. *Afraid* to see what the glass showed.

Sheed stepped out of the mirror's range, moved past Otto back to the end of the aisle.

"Sheed?" Otto said, chasing him. Not asking the obvious question. Instead, "Where are you going?"

"To get help. We need to finish what we started."

What was it Missus Nedraw said? The Bathroom Mirror Mass Communication System was the most advanced in the universe? Sheed found the aisle he'd passed earlier, the one exclusively for the sort of mirrors that go over sinks and resist getting foggy from shower steam. He stepped to the nearest mirror, trimmed in dull polished nickel, and stared at his reflection. He sensed Otto at his shoulder, keeping his distance, out of punching range.

"Missus Nedraw said *all it requires is a name and desire,*" Sheed sang to himself. "So how exactly does that work?"

Himself answered. Or his reflection did. "Who would you like to call?"

Sheed yelped and leapt backwards. His reflection did not move. It remained fixed within the mirror's frame, wearing a patient expression—the total opposite of everything Sheed was feeling. It repeated, "Who would you like to call?"

"Ummmm . . ."

"Sheed," Otto shouted for what felt like the hundredth time, "I saw something at the front of the emporium."

"I don't want to speak to *you* right now, Otto."

Still, Otto made the dangerous move of getting closer. "I know, but what I saw—"

"Leen Ellison!" Sheed yelled at the mirror.

Otto's head whipped between Sheed and his reflection. "What are you doing?"

The reflection swirled away, revealing a view like something from a hidden camera. They were peering into a bathroom, the strangest one they'd ever seen. Because it was completely underwater.

(Though there was that one time they'd defeated the vicious Gremlin King by cramming him down Grandma's toilet, but what happened then was still only, like, half underwater.)

There was wallpaper very unlike the tranquil starfish-and-seashell-patterned paper in Grandma's bathroom. The pattern here seemed to be shovels and human feet and *tractor tires?*

A towel rack was visible; instead of towels, wide sheets of seaweed wrapped around the bar and wavered with a gentle current. Due to the size of the mirror, there wasn't much to see beyond that. Though, at the leftmost border, something flicked just out of view. It looked like a fish tail.

Otto whispered, fearing what might happen next. "That's not our Leen."

"I don't care." Sheed knocked on the mirror like Missus Nedraw had done to him.

There was a sudden stillness in the frame. Then a churn of bubbles as a figure darted into view.

High-pitched but understandable, the being on the other side of the mirror said, "What are you?"

Even in the high tones of what was apparently Wet World speech, Otto recognized the creature.

Wiki. Ellison.

The Wet World version.

And she was a dolphin.

22

Go with the Flow

DOLPHIN WIKI STILL BORE a strong resemblance to the Human Wiki they were used to. Her ponytail fluttered in the quiet current of the underwater bathroom. She wore a flannel shirt fitted to her fins and cylindrical body. She stared Otto down with the disdain that seemed to be her constant in every dimension.

She twisted her beak away and yelled, "Leen! Get in here!"

A moment later, the edge of an open door swung into frame, before another dolphin skirted into the bathroom, flicking the door closed with her tail. Dolphin Leen bobbed into view next to her sister. Same short haircut the boys were familiar with. A flowy dress that undulated like the body of a jellyfish. She spotted the boys in the mirror and said, "Whoa. Interesting. What are they?"

Wiki did something with her fins that might translate to a shrug.

Leen asked the boys directly. "What are you?"

"We're humans," Otto squeaked.

"Hu . . . man?" Leen squinted. "You look a little bit like turtles without shells."

Sheed touched his chest. "Hey, Leen, you know us. I'm Sheed, and he's Otto. We're the Legendary Alstons."

The sisters looked to each other and laughed, but in the high cackling echoes—*kak-kak-ka-ka-ka-ka*—that the boys knew as dolphin calls because of documentaries and stuff.

The Ellisons' laughter ceased abruptly. Leen said, "Non-sense. My Sheed is a very handsome seahorse."

"I am?" Sheed grinned for reasons Otto couldn't begin to understand.

Wiki said, "And Otto is a prickly pufferfish."

"I'm a what?!"

"Though . . ." Wiki nudged closer to the mirror. "Your face. Even when compared to our Pufferfish Otto, you share—"

"Thirty-two identical facial characteristics," said Otto, "I know, I know. Just like I know about your photographic memory and Leen's crazy robots."

Leen said, "I haven't had a robot go crazy in a long time."

"Yesterday," said Wiki.

"I haven't had a robot go crazy since yesterday."

Wiki said, "I guess you are telling the truth. Which leads me to deduce you're from another dimension. Based on all the mirrors behind you, plus the fact that you're speaking to us through a mirror, suggests you're in that weird mirror emporium downtown."

Sheed grinned, impressed.

Otto mumbled, "I hate you."

Wiki, mischievous, said, "You *are* like my cranky little pufferfish." *Kak-kak-ka-ka-ka-ka*. "So, you need our help, right?"

"You don't have to stick your snout in the air like that when you say it."

"The correct term is rostrum, not snout. And yes I do."

Sheed could tell Otto would keep arguing, and cut him off. "We need your help."

The Ellisons rotated toward each other, beaks—er, *rostrums*—nearly touching. Even though their dolphin expressions were limited, Otto imagined them communicating a silent "we knew it" to one another.

"How can we be of assistance?" the sisters said at once.

Otto begrudgingly said, "We need to get back to Warped World."

"What's a Warped World?" said Leen, expelling bubbles from her blowhole.

Otto recapped all that had happened that afternoon. From their first contact with Missus Nedraw, to their first trip through a mirror, to the strangeness of Warped World, to now.

"This Nevan guy locked the mirror we came through, so we can't get back."

Wiki *ka-ka*'d. "You can't get back the way you came."

"That's what I said."

"Oh dear, I assumed your extremely swollen cranium meant you'd have a bigger brain than the pufferfish I spend so much time bailing out. Sadly, that does not appear to be the case. I guess every Otto, in every dimension, needs a me."

Otto screwed up his face, ready to say something harsh and likely inadequate, but Sheed stepped in front of him, yet again interrupting a typically petty Otto and Wiki argument. "We're listening, Wiki."

"All the mirrors you saw lead to a version of the emporium in a different world, right?"

"Right," the boys said together.

"But the mirror that directly connects our world to this 'Warped World' has become inaccessible."

"Right."

"So take a detour."

Otto blinked slowly. Resisted the urge to smack himself in the forehead. Was it really that simple?

He whipped out his notebook.

ENTRY #69

(It must be noted that I would've
come to this on my own eventually without Wiki's help, thank you.) Every one
of those mirrors leads to a different
version of the emporium. Nevan and his
cronies blocked the one that connects
Warped World and Wet World. But would
they have blocked all the others?

DEDUCTION: Unlikely. There were hundreds.
That means if we take a different
mirror, to a different emporium, we only

182

have to find one that leads back to
Warped World and isn't blocked.

Otto sighed.

Further DEDUCTION: That might take a
while. Some of the mirrors might be
quite dangerous.

What other option did they have?

Dolphin Wiki said, "We're getting tired of watching you scribble, Octavius."

Dolphin Leen said, "Especially since Hu-Man Sheed seems so sad. Or do hu-man faces look like that all the time?"

"I'm fine," Sheed said.

Was he? The Black Mirror . . .

Otto forced himself to focus on the problem at hand. First Warped World, then they'd deal with whatever Sheed saw back there. "We're going to have to do some mirror jumping. I think we should walk the interdimensional mirror aisle and closely examine the frames. Those seem to indicate the particular characteristics of the worlds they take us to. We can try to determine which frames look safest and stick to those."

"That could take forever," Sheed said.

"Maybe. But if we find a good five or six we feel comfortable with, then we'll already have options when we reach the next emporium."

Our biggest problem is the order of
the mirrors isn't the same in every
emporium, apparently. In our world, the
Warped World mirror was the last on
the left, here it was right smack in
the middle of a thousand other mirror
options. We'll have to find it among the
others, wherever we end up.

DEDUCTION: We'll be very, very thorough
in identifying good mirrors while we're
here. It may take time, but it's the
safest plan. Well worth it.

While Otto thought through the most logical way to
approach the task, Sheed, who'd finally noticed the ticking timers mounted about the emporium, asked the girls,
"What's up with all these clocks counting down?"

On the wall to their left, the digits ticked.

00:05:25

00:05:24

00:05:23

Dolphin Leen said, "That's just the time until High
Tide."

"Oh." Sheed glanced at the clock, still ticking down,

and said, "I feel like, I don't know—I feel like that's important in a way you're probably not explaining."

Dolphin Wiki said, "Guys, your world can't be that different from ours. Don't tell me you shop during Low Tide where you're from."

Otto's chin tilted up then, a concerned look on his face. "High and Low Tide isn't really a factor in our shopping routines. Please elaborate."

Both girls spewed pluming bubbles, totally surprised. "Stores here close at Low Tide and open at High Tide."

Open?

"Oh snap!" said Sheed.

Otto spun slowly in space, taking in the drips, and puddles, and various dampnesses of the place. Everything was wet, but from what? "Are you saying at Low Tide stores close here, and the water is drained out?"

"Yes," said Wiki. "Saves money on water conditioning bills."

Otto didn't know what water conditioning was and figured it was the least of his concerns. "So, when stores open, the water . . ."

Dolphin Leen said, "Comes rushing back in with crushing force." *Kak-kak-ka-ka-ka-ka.*

00:03:59

00:03:58

00:03:57

23

00:03:56

"HEY, WHERE ARE YOU GUYS GOING?" Dolphin Leen called.

Dolphin Wiki said, "Not even a thank-you, huh?"

"Thanks!!" the boys shouted, rounding the corner on the run.

They darted down the aisle of interdimensional mirrors. Sheed said, "What are we looking for?"

"A mirror in a frame that doesn't look dangerous."

Should've been easy. All those mirrors, there had to be a fair number of clearly safe options. Wellll . . .

The frame made of bones and shrieking skulls didn't feel encouraging.

Nor did the frame that made it look like the mirror was wedged into a dragon's jaws.

00:02:11

00:02:10

00:02:09

They'd passed three or four dozen mirrors. The red serpent eyeball frame. The frame that was plain except for the words *Acid Burn* repeated over and over graffiti style. The cyclops-ogre frame. All bad.

00:01:01

00:01:00

00:00:59

Screeching static squawked through unseen speakers before morphing into cheery uptempo jazz. Shopping music. Opening time was near.

"We gotta get outta here!" Sheed kept running. Kept looking for a safe mirror.

"You think?" Otto was on his heels.

00:00:32

00:00:31

00:00:30

Metal groaned. Above them, the mouths of large pipes suspended from the ceiling groaned open.

Sheed skidded to a stop. "What about this one?"

The frame was like a child's drawing of the sky. A pretty blue, big bright yellow sun at the top. Cartoonishly green grass at the bottom. It seemed rather pleasant.

"What kind of world is it, though?" Otto said, skeptical.

"It don't matter. We're out of time."

Sheed was not wrong.

00:00:03

00:00:02

00:00:01

The pipes, hundreds of them, spewed blue gouts of water in near-solid columns all over the emporium. The sudden liquid explosion created ten-foot waves on either end of the aisle, rushing at them like two walls set to smoosh the boys between them.

"Maneuver #23!" they shouted at each other. *Just do it!*

Otto and Sheed leapt through the mirror as the walls of water smashed together in the space they'd occupied seconds before.

They experienced that strange, barely-there resistance of pushing through the glass. An instant later, they were

spit out the other side onto lush green grass that smelled like springtime. Their clothes had changed from wetsuits to shorts and T-shirts, attire they'd wear on any warm day. Standing, they noted this was definitely still a mirror emporium, but one quite different from any they'd seen so far.

The shelves housing the mirrors weren't metal slats connected with nuts and bolts, but crooked and veiny branches, like tree limbs. Over their heads, thick foliage meant the ceiling was only visible through gaps in closely bunched leaves, and the lighting looked more like sunshine than something from a bulb. The chittering call of some unknown bird echoed.

"You know what this place is?" Otto said.

"Warm World," said Sheed.

Otto's face scrunched. "I was going to say *Wild* World, but okay."

"Man, whatever. Let's find the Warped World mirror. I'm going this way." He stomped off, pointed in the opposite direction. "You go that way. Yell if you find it first."

"I don't think we should split up."

"You aren't my boss, Otto."

Otto bit back a sharp response. Fighting wasn't going to be helpful right now.

So, he trekked off and away from Sheed. Even though Otto had decided not to fight, it didn't stop him from getting angrier and angrier (and maybe a little sadder). He couldn't decide those feelings away.

He focused on the mirrors.

Sheed was not focused on the mirrors. He tried, glancing at maybe every other frame, hoping to recognize one that would take them back to Warped World. But he kept feeling . . . hollow. Empty. Except for the anger he felt over Otto keeping such a big secret.

Now you have a secret, that Grandma-like voice in his head reminded him. He'd looked into the Black Mirror and knew the one thing Otto didn't. How much time he had left.

That secret made him forget his mission of finding a suitable mirror for their next jump. He reached the end of the aisle—a long, long walk—and hadn't identified a single one. Heck, he'd barely even seen them. His own day-before-his-death reflection was the most prominent vision in his head.

He prepared to double back, to actually do his job this time. The growl stopped him.

The foliage over the main corridor created deep shadows where the sound seeped from. In those shadows, a pair of red eyes glowed.

Sheed ran back the way he'd come, yelling, "Warm World has pets!"

He sprinted toward Otto, as did the thing chasing him. It wasn't clear what sort of animal it was, but quick glances over his shoulder confirmed it sure had a lot of teeth.

"Tell me you found a mirror!" Sheed shouted.

Not exactly. There were some low possibilities. The mirror with the frame made up entirely of doll heads seemed a better choice than the frame depicting a black hole. But that didn't make it ideal. Because . . . doll heads.

Otto spun in a circle, trying to gauge which of the frames would be the best of his potentially bad choices.

Ski mask and machete frame? Nope.

Terrifying robot frame? Probably not.

Icicle and earmuffs? Hmmmm.

"You better pick fast," Sheed said, almost on him. The snarling beast gaining.

"From warm to cold," Otto mumbled, grabbing Sheed's shirt and dragging him through their next mirror.

They plopped through, landing face first in a foot of crisp snow.

The boys pushed themselves up on their knees; they were now clad in thick parkas with hoods and fur lining.

"Winter World?" Sheed said, trying the designation on for size.

"Works for me," said Otto.

They scanned the aisle of mirrors, used to the constant similarities of each emporium, while taking in the big differences (the shelves here were made of solid carved ice). There was a stillness to this chilly emporium . . . no immediate danger detected, but they were already shivering despite the cold-weather gear they'd gained on the trip.

"We . . . can't," Otto began, his chattering teeth

chomping his sentence into bite-size segments, "stay here for . . . long."

Sheed agreed. "We'll freeze."

So the search began in earnest, with the temperature seeming to plummet every minute they were there. Unable to find the clown-framed funhouse mirror that would take them back to Warped World before tiny icicles began forming in their eyebrows, Otto and Sheed opted for an early jump through a mirror with a frame made of orange, brown, and rust-colored leaves.

This brought them into a perfectly temperate emporium —their outfits in this world were thin jackets and jeans. This should've allowed for a more leisurely search, but tiny hurricanes began developing, forcing them to make another leap through a pink mirror that spat them into an emporium constructed entirely of cotton candy. Then the next frame, one made of stone, put them in a world that excited Otto greatly.

He said, "Dude, we're dinosaurs. Judging by the plates running up your back, you're a—"

"Shut. Up. Otto!"

They leapt again.

This pattern repeated a dozen times, a forced leap through a seemingly safe mirror only to arrive in a place that ranged from intolerably inconvenient (it's hard to walk on cotton candy) to outright deadly until, finally, in an emporium made of giant, looming dominoes, they found the Warped World mirror.

They stood before it, staring at their weirdly warbling reflections in the distorted glass. Neither seemed anxious to make a move.

"We should talk before we go through," Sheed said.

"Yes. We don't know what will be waiting on the other side. We should be ready for a fight."

"Yeah. That, too. But I meant I should tell you about the Black Mirror."

Otto had been jittery and anxious over the potential of running smack-dab into Nevan, his Jurors, and the spiders. Sheed's sudden willingness to share amplified both sensations. "Okay," he said, though it didn't feel okay.

"I looked a little older," Sheed said, sounding like a robot. "I had some hair on my face. Maybe three or four years from now."

"Three—" Otto couldn't get the second word up, was too busy holding back a sudden, barely controllable sob.

Sheed said, "It was hard to tell because I was really thin. I *looked* sick."

Otto's throat felt tight, still he said, "Sheed, that reflection doesn't have to be true."

"That's not what TimeStar—I mean *you*—said, right?"

"We can fix it." Otto thought of the stolen vial still in his pocket. "In Warped World. The medicine."

"You know it will work? For sure?"

"No. Not for sure. Probably. But . . ." Otto shook his head. No lies here. Too important. "Dr. Medina said she wouldn't give it to you unless you stayed in Warped World forever. There might be side effects."

Sheed's head wrenched Otto's way. "Like what?"

"It's unclear."

Sheed laughed then. Full on, chin to the ceiling, gut-busting laughter.

Otto flinched. "You're being scary."

"I'm sorry," Sheed said, the laughs subsiding. "I am. I shouldn't have been mad at you for keeping it to yourself. Knowing sucks. You dealt with that suckage by yourself for weeks, and I'm sorry for that, too."

"We can still figure something out. Okay? Don't give up."

"Give up? Three or four years is a long time. We got a lot of fights to get through. Starting now. Let's do it." Sheed took a step toward the Warped World mirror, but Otto grabbed his sleeve.

"Are you sure you're okay?"

"Solid, cuzzo. No worries."

Otto *was* worried. Sheed didn't really *seem* okay, though Otto couldn't really tell what felt off. Sheed had laughed. He said he was ready for a fight. What was he feeling, though? Grandma often said you can't really tell what a person has going on inside them. People cover up their fears but don't always think straight when they're scared.

The emporium they were in was stable. No immediate danger around. *Maybe me and Sheed should talk some more,* Otto thought. *Before making the jump to Warped—*

Sheed leapt through the mirror.

Well, dang.

Otto followed.

He emerged on the other side prepared for battle. Fortunately, the aisle was completely deserted, though voices flitted from the front of the emporium. Nevan and his crew hadn't strayed far.

This was a good thing, though. Time to evaluate the situation, form a plan.

The first thing Otto evaluated was himself. Returning to Warped World had put them back in their original clothing and reactivated Otto's physical fluctuation—to use Dr. Medina's expression. His skin had become the impossibly strong rock that had helped them escape before. Big difference: the rockiness had spread. It now covered his face, confirmed by a quick glance at a mirror across the aisle. Also his feet, which had swelled and burst through his sneakers.

He dug in his pocket, fishing out the vial of Fixityall that had gone clear when they left Warped World. It was back to its natural (if you could call such an elixir natural) state of glowing yellow. Even with the talk of side effects and Sheed having to stay in Warped World, making the use of the medicine unlikely, Otto's spirit was lifted by the option of it.

"We should talk about this medicine more," Otto said, turning to Sheed, "because—ACK!"

"What?" Sheed asked, yet to check a mirror.

"Your face."

"What about my—" He checked the nearest mirror. "ACK!"

Sheed's face was gone. Erased by another Warped World physical fluctuation.

No cheeks. No lips. No forehead.

His 'fro and his trusty pick were still intact, though. That offered little comfort.

A pristine Afro on a clean, bleached-white skull just wasn't a great look.

Not even for Sheed.

24

The Morty Look

BACK AT D. FRANKLIN MIDDLE SCHOOL, in Mr. Rickard's science room, there was a skeleton named Morty who usually got some sort of makeover around Halloween. It's been a DFMS October tradition to dress Morty up in three-piece suits or a leather jacket. It wasn't unusual for the skeleton to get accessorized with sunglasses or a hat.

In that moment, if someone had swapped Skull-Faced Sheed for Halloween Morty, a casual observer might have had a tough time telling them apart. It was a little too much for the usually cool-under-pressure Sheed to take. His knees buckled. Otto jumped forward to catch him before he fell.

"Whoa, whoa, whoa," Otto said. He lifted Sheed off the ground and couldn't tell if it was his new rocky strength or Sheed's sudden lack of flesh that made his cousin so light.

"I'm fine," Sheed said, "just a little shook from the trip."

He pushed at Otto's chest with bony fingers that were as bare and white as his face.

Otto set him down. "Does it hurt?"

"Does being a walking, talking rock hurt?"

No. It didn't. That didn't mean Sheed had actually answered his question either.

"Come on," said Sheed, "what's the plan here?

A gruff Nevan continued to speak loudly, with authority, near the entrance of the emporium. They were too far away to make out any of his words, though.

"We should sneak a little closer. Try to see what he's talking about. Could be important."

"Lead the way."

Otto took a step—a clunky, loud, lumbering step. A rock foot on a concrete floor did not make for stealthy approach. "Dude, I can't sneak."

"Wait here." Sheed yanked up the hood of his coat, cinched the drawstring so it constricted tight around his face, giving him a look similar to the Grim Reaper. "I got this."

He skittered around the corner, feeling nearly weightless in his new form. As he moved closer to Nevan and company, he ran his bony hands across his chest and stomach. Awesome! They were still there. It was only his face and hands missing flesh.

But would the condition spread like Otto's? Why was it happening at all?

A few mirror rows from Nevan's gathering, Sheed slunk into the shadows, straining to listen, peering through the gaps in the shelves for a limited view of all present.

The sloth Juror with the fancy fingernails held a notebook before her. "After a cursory review of Evian Nedraw's logs, I see that insane Executioner of yours has been imposing his unique brand of justice on the residents of this world for some time. There are several dozen of his prisoners here in the emporium."

Nevan bounced around, his heavy body shaking the foundation. "Interesting. Now that I've reclaimed my role in overseeing all of the emporiums across the various realms, we should reach out to the highest powers in this world to settle the matter of prisoner accommodations."

The Jurors mumbled agreement, but Spencer didn't seem all that clear on the instruction. "You mean like a president or king? So we can get permission to release the wrongly imprisoned?"

Nevan's voice was syrupy sweet. "I was thinking more like a banker or treasurer."

Harvey Hippo said, "Because they can pay us."

"Harvey," Nevan said, "we've been over this."

Harvey shut his big mouth.

"I don't know much about that part of it, mate," said Spencer. "Can't we just let the people go like you did for us?"

Nevan said, "That was a situation of imminent danger. When Evie Nedraw and my Executioner were still on the loose. Now that they've been apprehended, there's a certain order to these things. Don't worry, we'll release the innocent. Just *after* we talk to a banker or a treasurer."

Spencer crossed his six arms, obviously unsatisfied. Nevan leaned in, placing a comforting hand on one of the spider's shoulder and giving Sheed a better view of him.

Sheed gasped.

Nevan was more huge, more muscular (still with that tiny head) than before. The jewelry he'd been rocking hadn't adjusted to his new form. It was too tight, embedded in his flesh like it was a part of him. He caressed the gold chain that looked etched into his collarbone and said, "Don't worry, friend. I have every intention of making things right here."

Sheed didn't like the sound of that at all. He slid around the shelving closest to him onto the next aisle, which was less organized. More like loose storage for a number of randomly sized mirrors. Moving past one, he detected motion from the corner of his eye and clamped a bony hand over his bony mouth to prevent a yelp.

The Judge—Sheed felt way more comfortable granting him that title over Executioner—loomed hulking and silent in his glass cage. His shoulders heaved with each breath, but he didn't move otherwise. Backing up a step, Sheed checked other mirrors stored along with the Judge's. Sure enough, just a few feet away, was Missus Nedraw's.

She was much more animated in her cell than the Judge. Mouthing things and pointing frantically. Sheed couldn't understand what she was trying to say, so he whispered, "Slow down."

Her fists clenched and she took deep breaths. Moving her lips slowly, she mouthed, *Emergency exit,* while pointing the way Sheed had come from.

"Where exactly?" he whispered.

She pointed down, then shoved her palms toward Sheed in a pushing motion.

Her mirror rested on a wheeled trolley. Sheed grabbed

her frame and tugged, testing the ease of movement and noise. The wheels turned with barely a hiss.

He began wheeling her to where Otto waited, but she made more jerky pointing motions and mouthed, extra slowly, *Get the Law.*

Following her pointer finger, Sheed spotted the Judge's large legal manual tossed carelessly on the floor across the aisle.

Sheed grabbed the heavy volume, wedged it onto the wheeled platform, and moved. It wasn't hard work exactly, yet by the time he turned to the corner and found Otto waiting, his arms and legs burned; he struggled to catch his breath.

Otto met him halfway, unsure how Sheed had gotten Missus Nedraw away from Nevan, but sensing she might be useful in whatever came next. Provided they could escape the emporium.

"Emergency," Sheed said, gulping air, "exit. Somewhere."

Missus Nedraw gestured toward the absolute backside of the emporium.

Otto picked her mirror up, tucked it under one arm. Sheed grabbed the Law. They delved deeper into the mirror maze. Every so often, Otto flipped the mirror around to look Missus Nedraw in the face, and she'd point in another direction. They finally reached a back corner of the vast emporium. There—a three-way mirror like the kind in dressing rooms when Grandma had them try on new clothes at the mall.

"This it?" Sheed asked.

Missus Nedraw nodded vigorously.

"Is this going to take us to another world?" Otto asked.

Missus Nedraw shook her head. No, then. They'd still be in Warped World.

Otto said, "*Where* will it take us?"

What she mouthed then, neither boy could make out, even though she said it three times.

They hesitated until an echoing voice bounced their way. Nevan's. "Nedraw's gone! Find her."

Time was up.

Sheed went first, taking the Law. Otto passed through second, carrying Missus Nedraw's mirror. They emerged in a place both familiar and surprising.

25

Joyful Noise

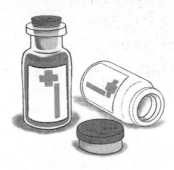

THE EMERGENCY EXIT MIRROR spat them out into what the boys first thought was another emporium. It was dark, and there were shelves, but a quick examination revealed not mirrors, but tools. And lawnmowers. And rolls of duct tape, among other items.

"This is Mr. Archie's hardware store," Sheed said, before sneezing from all the dust.

The light bulbs over their heads were broken, so they could barely see their surroundings. Even their own reflections were dark silhouettes in the mirror they'd come through. What little light there was came from afternoon sun beaming between boards fixed over the front windows. No one had set foot in this place in a long time.

Otto held Missus Nedraw's mirror at arm's length for a face-to-face talk. "Where's Mr. Archie, and Anna?"

Missus Nedraw, still mute on her side of the glass, mouthed, *Emporium*.

"The Judge got them, too?" An angry edge crept into Otto's voice.

Free me, she mouthed next, dodging the question.

Otto raised the mirror high, intending to slam it on the ground to shatter the glass and free the warden. Sheed touched his arm, stopping him. "It wasn't just the Judge. She helped."

Missus Nedraw pounded on her side of the glass. *Free me.*

"No," said Sheed. "Put her down and come here."

Otto spun Missus Nedraw toward the wall and leaned her mirror against it so she couldn't see them. To Sheed, he said, "What's the maneuver? What are we doing?"

"Nevan's got big plans for Warped World. It ain't good, cuzzo."

"He really is a nightmare." Otto stroked his chin, his rock-on-rock flesh making a clunking sound. "The Judge doesn't seem much better, though."

Sheed made a show of looking around the Archie's Hardware Store that didn't have any Archies. "We need help, Otto."

"Wiki and Leen?"

"No. Not this time. Someone's gotta be out there to fight if we mess this up."

Otto agreed and was relieved. He was not up for more of Wiki's gloating. "Who, then?"

"You know where we're supposed to go if we're ever in real trouble."

Otto's rocky shoulders slumped. "That might not be a great idea."

"I want to see her, Otto. Just let me call the shots for once. Please."

Sheed said please. And meant it. Fine. "Can you get us there?"

"Provided Warped World cooperates, I think so."

"Lead the way."

Much like Grandma on any given Sunday, Sheed took them to church.

The whole town of Fry felt deserted. The random and terrifying changes that they'd grown to expect during their time in Warped World were fewer and less extreme as they moved. Otto still carried Missus Nedraw in her mirror, and Sheed toted the Law.

During the last quarter mile of walking, they heard the church before they saw it. The closer they got, the louder it became, the joyful noise of a dozen voices attempting a single harmony. They crested the hill and spotted the building, an island surrounded by a sea of grass, the sweet singing inside swelling to a crescendo. Of course it was this world's Grandma and her choirmates, but if you didn't know better, you might suspect the tiny white-and-bird's-egg-blue building of having its own voice.

One of the double doors was propped open, allowing a breeze in, just like back home. The boys hesitated at the steps leading to it.

"Should we just go in like this?" Otto glanced down at his swollen, granite form.

Sheed's skeletal jaw flapped in a way that didn't seem to sync up with his words. "Grandma always said this was the one place where you could come as you are." He took the steps first. "We are."

Otto followed his cousin across the threshold into an entrance hall that was identical to the one he knew. He was suddenly so, so homesick.

Sheed pressed his palm against the door leading into the sanctuary and nudged his way into the choir rehearsal. The singing continued, the ladies barely noticing their guests. They were all in their sections — sopranos and altos — with the choir director, Miss Eloise, giving them cues, her wide teal hat swaying in time with her elaborate hand motions.

Otto wasn't used to seeing Grandma and the other ladies in their church hats — their "crowns" — with the bold colors matching whatever dress they wore and brims wider than their shoulders *at rehearsal*. Dressing so fancy when it wasn't even Sunday felt odd until Miss Eloise said, "Altos, go higher."

Nothing about the alto section voices changed, though.

Wings unfurled from their hats, fluffy with bright feathers, flapping powerfully, lifting the women a few inches above the other sections.

"Good, good," Miss Eloise said.

Otto leaned into Sheed. "Now what? How do we convince her to help?"

Sheed craned his neck, and Otto heard the firecracker pops of the bones. "Same thing we always say when we need her." Then Sheed shouted, "Grandma!"

The singing came to an abrupt halt. The wings from Grandma's hat snapped taut, and in two mighty flaps, she flew from her place in the choir stand to hover a few feet from the boys, her hat-wings working in such a frenzy they blurred like a hummingbird's.

What was a sheer expression of panic shifted into something like confusion when she saw the boys. "Oh sweet Lord, for a second I thought I heard my grandsons."

"No," said Otto, "we're just strange visitors from—"

Sheed cut him off. "It's us, Grandma. Not this world's version . . . That Otto and Sheed need your help, too. We came to you because we didn't know where else to go."

There was a buffeting of air as another dozen pairs of wings flapped, bringing all of the Church Ladies in close, all hovering and on guard.

"What's all this about?" asked Miss Eloise.

Grandma was slow answering, examining the boys with an extreme squint. Her eyes widened, and any questions she might've had about who they claimed to be and where they might be from became less important. "These are my grandbabies," she said to Miss Eloise. "Somehow."

One of the altos pointed at Sheed. "How can you tell? That one don't have a face."

"A grandma knows! Now, what brought you here, children? Is it about the disappearances around town?"

Otto said, "Yes, Grandma. It is. We have someone who can help us get to the bottom of it." He turned Missus Nedraw's mirror around for all to see. The warden sulked on her side of the glass. Otto propped the mirror against a wall and drew back his rocky fist. "Stand back. I'm going to break it and let her out."

The Church Ladies hovered back a few yards, while Sheed ducked behind a pew with the Law.

Otto punched the glass. Instead of the fantastic shattering he'd expected, a weird warbling sounded, echoing throughout the sanctuary as his fist rebounded. The glass didn't even crack.

Missus Nedraw shook her head, mouthed, *Maximum security.*

So the glass was tougher. What now?

Grandma fluttered next to him, examining the mirror cell. "Step away and let us try. Ladies."

They all joined, still hovering inches above the ground, but in similar formation as when they were in the choir stand. Miss Eloise, still directing, said, "On three. One, and two, and . . ."

The choir sang. Not a song. A long, high, sustained note that shifted, and sharpened until Otto and Sheed had to cup hands over their ears. Missus Nedraw's mirror vibrated with the changing sound until a series of hairline cracks began to crawl from the edge of the frame to the center, then—

The mirror shattered, and Missus Nedraw ejected from the frame, somersaulting and landing in a crouch. She maintained the position while she blew a loose strand of hair aside with a puff of breath. Standing, she smoothed the wrinkles in her outfit, then faced the Church Ladies. "Thank you for your assistance. Your cooperation will be noted in my report of today's incidents."

Grandma said, "You'll forgive us if we aren't gushing with gratitude. What's going on with my grandchildren?"

"I am . . . unsure."

Sheed said, "Let me clear it up for you. Your boss tossed them and a bunch of other people into a mirror."

"Well, then, they *must've* broken the law."

Grandma slapped Missus Nedraw in the back of the head. "The devil is a lie."

Missus Nedraw pursed her lips, but made the smart and brave decision to stay quiet.

Otto said, "You were right about Nevan being a bad guy. Your boss ain't all that, either."

Missus Nedraw, wary, took two big steps out of Grandma's smacking range before speaking. "I am not always a fan of his methods, but he saw the corruption in Nevan and his Jury before anyone else. He took action to restore my society, and the societies across the various worlds in which Nevan had profited from the emporiums, to a state of order. When he recruited me eight years ago, he assured me whatever rulings he made would be based upon the letter of the Law. That was fair, even though it sometimes can seem harsh."

"But he didn't stop expanding the emporiums, did he? You opened shop in our world a year ago. You came here to Warped World a little before that."

"Those were plans Nevan had already initiated. We just saw them to fruition so we could make sure they were done the right way. Done according to—"

"The Law," Sheed said, disgusted. He threw the heavy volume she'd insisted he take from the emporium at her feet.

Grandma said, "Those are *your* laws. Not ours. *You* have to obey. To force it on us, to tell us the way we live and enjoy our lives is wrong . . . That's what a tyrant does."

The Church Ladies grunted in agreement. Miss Eloise let out an extended "Amennnnn."

Missus Nedraw became flustered. Her explanation wasn't getting through.

"On the day the Judge handed me the keys to the emporium, he swore on this very book that he would never allow himself to become corrupt the way Nevan had. He would not be bought, or fooled." She snatched up the Law and said, "He promised me all of his decisions would be clear interpretations of the writings within. The statutes and ordinances and various rules are meant to protect us. You'll see, it's not malicious. It's meant to make lives better through order."

She dropped the book on a nearby pew, flipped the front cover open, and stiffened.

Otto, Sheed, the Church Ladies waited.

Missus Nedraw flipped a few pages. Then turned to the midpoint of the legal manual. Then she flipped all the way to the end, before riffling through pages at random, more desperate by the second. Her breathing quickened, and her eyes glistened with tears.

"No," she whispered, "this can't be right."

Otto and Sheed drew closer, flanking Missus Nedraw. They got a glimpse of the book and understood why the warden was so devastated.

The Law, the book that the Judge had lorded over her, and used to encourage her unquestioning obedience, its pages . . .

Were blank.

26
Evian's Reveal

ENTRY #79

Nevan is corrupt and can be bought.
The Judge is insane and makes up his
own rules. They're both horrible, and
powerful.

DEDUCTION: For the sake of Warped
World—and every other world they
can reach through the mirrors in the
emporium—we gotta stop them. But—

OTTO FUMBLED HIS TINY PENCIL. His stubby, rocky
fingers were proving a hindrance to accurate record keeping again. It fell and rolled under a nearby pew, making it
impossible for him to reach unless he ripped the bench from

its floor bolts—something he imagined the Church Ladies wouldn't be happy about.

"Sheed," Otto said.

"Huh—wha?" Sheed had curled up on a pew, rested his head on Grandma's lap, and dozed off. When Otto's voice roused him, he was slow rising, and his bones crackled like they were brittle.

"Can you grab my pencil?"

Sheed moved like a slug, groaning when he knelt, and making little whimpering sounds as he searched beneath the pew. He found the pencil, but the short walk to return it to Otto was quite tiring. He even felt a little nauseous, which was strange, since he wasn't completely sure he still had a stomach. He'd become more of a skeleton in just the last hour.

Grandma watched them both struggle in their new conditions. "You two aren't normally like this, are you? How did you get this way?"

"A doctor told us it's a 'physical fluctuation' and it's normal and unpredictable. For here. I guess," said Otto.

Sheed simply nodded.

"You know," Grandma said, "the doctor ain't wrong, change is normal here, but it's not some fickle thing. Your bodies are doing what they're doing for a reason. I watched it happen with my boys—the ones from here, I mean."

Sheed held up his bony hand. "I'm going to die, so this makes sense."

Grandma flinched. "You're going to what, now?"

"Long story."

"One that doesn't have to end the way you think," Otto said, angry. He stomped to his cousin, the church floor groaning under his weight.

"Because of the magic medicine I can't take unless I stay here?"

"Yes!" Otto shouted, and even his voice sounded like his throat was coated in gravel. Almost a roar.

The Church Ladies fluttered over in a rush, cutting their eyes at the boys. "Now, I know y'all know better than to be shouting up in here."

"They do," said Grandma. "Act like you got some home training."

"Yes, Grandma," they said in unison.

While the how-to-handle-Sheed's-sickness argument was far from over, attention turned to the other elephant in the room. The completely undone Missus Nedraw, who'd retreated to a corner, crouched, rocking herself in a failed attempt at some sort of comfort. The Judge's useless, blank manual tossed aside.

Sheed waved in her direction, a signal for Otto to focus. They approached her.

"Missus Nedraw?" Otto said.

She wouldn't meet their eyes. "You should just go home. Take the emergency exit back into the emporium, go through the mirror back to your world and forget about this place."

"No," Sheed said. "You brought us here to stop a dangerous fugitive."

"I was wrong, Rasheed. I see that everything they ever said about me was true."

"They who?"

"All of my doubters. My name is Evian—do you know what that spells backwards?"

Otto and Sheed thought on it a second. Got it at the same time. "Oh."

"*Naïve.* You may not know this, but the world the Judge, Nevan, and I come from can be quite stiff and rigid."

"No," Otto said, shaking his head way too fervently.

"Never would've guessed," said Sheed, droll.

Missus Nedraw went on. "When I started my path to a law career, I intended to right wrongs and help the helpless. My fellow law students would tease me so. 'Evian the Naïve will believe anything,' they'd say. 'She'd believe a snake if it told her it wasn't cold-blooded.'

"Then the Judge came into power, and those naysayers began to disappear because they 'violated THE LAW,' and I felt vindicated because I was free. I must've have been doing something right. The Judge recruited me to run the prisons, and I was so happy to be his second in command. His shining knight. I was his fool. I see that now. Why can't you?" She focused on Sheed. "Oh, right, you don't have eyes at the moment."

Sheed didn't, just empty sockets in his skull, but he still saw things just fine. Perhaps better than Missus Nedraw. "You may have been wrong about some things, but not Nevan. I heard his plan. He wants to get power and money, and he doesn't care who gets hurt. So, we go home, then what? Wait until he's strong enough to come to our world and do the same thing there?"

Otto said, "We need to stop him. Here and now."

"How?" Missus Nedraw said. "His Jurors are loyal, and he's convinced that spider gang—"

"They're not a gang. They're a dance crew."

"Whatever they are, they're with him."

Grandma flapped over, bobbing in the air. "I'll help. My grandbabies need me, then I'm there."

Miss Eloise and the rest of the Church Ladies joined in, their wings creating a mighty breeze. "*We'll* help too. It's what we do."

Missus Nedraw stood. Slowly. The bearer of bad news. "As wonderful as all this teamwork is, it's still not enough. The spiders alone. There's gotta be a hundred of them."

She wasn't wrong. Though, Sheed never got the impression ArachnoBRObia were in love with Nevan's schemes. They were grateful because he freed them, a courtesy they thought they were paying forward when they grabbed Otto and Sheed. They wanted to help. They were just helping the wrong dude. If only there was a way to make Spencer and his family see it.

Otto said, "Missus Nedraw, a more positive attitude would really be helpful right about now. I mean, maybe we can recruit some fighters. Get the town involved."

"You mean the ones the Judge hasn't crammed into a mirror yet? He already captured the bravest and strongest of this world on a whim. He did most of Nevan's job for him without even knowing it, and I helped." She began softly banging her forehead against the wall.

Miss Eloise said, "Ma'am, we just painted that wall."

Missus Nedraw spoke to no one in particular. "For eight years I believed him. Eight years of following blindly. I'm such a fool."

Sheed perked up. "*Eight* years?"

"Yes." She bounced her forehead off the wall— *THUNK*. "Eight"— *THUNK*—"years."

Sheed turned to Otto. "Eight years. Give me your notepad."

Without giving him time to comply, Sheed fished in Otto's pocket. Otto squirmed but didn't fight him. The first thing Sheed pulled out was the vial of Fixityall, which he stared at a moment. Hope in a bottle.

But Sheed didn't like the conditions of that hope, so he pushed the vial at Otto's chest, letting it go before his cousin even had a good grip.

"Hey!" Otto said, fumbling the bottle, catching it

before it fell to the floor, possibly shattering. While he was distracted with that, Sheed riffled through Otto's writings.

"You were taking notes when we were underground with Nevan and ArachnoBRObia. Which entries are those?"

"Somewhere between #55 and #65, I think. What are you looking for?"

Sheed didn't answer, too busy skimming Otto's precise handwriting, until—"Got it! Yes!"

"What is it?" Otto asked, but Sheed bypassed him in favor of Missus Nedraw.

"Look at this!" Sheed said, shoving the pad at the warden.

"It's a tiny notebook."

"Read it." Sheed tapped the page with bare-bone finger. "Here."

She did. Once. Twice. A third time. Suddenly, she wasn't so downtrodden. Her back straightened, and her jaw clenched. "Wait. That means . . ."

Otto leaned in, checking his own notes, and it dawned on him, too. He thought back to when Nevan was mono-loguing earlier, before the trip to Wet World. When he'd stumbled over the word *eight*. "Oh. Ohhhhh."

Grandma said, "You mind filling the rest of us in on all the excitement?"

"Spencer, our spider friend, and his dance crew were knocked out and thrown in a mirror ten years go. They believed the Judge did it. But Nevan and his Jurors were in power until eight years ago, when the Judge snapped and locked them away. That means—"

"The spiders were locked up on Nevan's watch," Missus Nedraw said. "Of course. I'd never considered they didn't know."

Otto said, "Spencer and his crew are working for their jailor without knowing it."

"We can maybe shift the fight in our favor," said Sheed.

Missus Nedraw sagged, literally deflating before their eyes. "That's very risky. Maybe the risk isn't worth it. Not in this crazy world." Her cheeks sank; her clothes became baggy. Sheed threw his hands up, flustered. But Missus Nedraw's sudden physical fluctuation tickled the back of Otto's brain.

Otto retrieved his pad and pinched his pencil between his stony thumb and forefinger.

ENTRY #80

Missus Nedraw told us this world was unpredictable. Illogical. Dangerous. So when I started turning to stone and Sheed became a skeleton, we thought it was random. In the moment. But every strange thing we've seen has fit the people we've met.

· Mr. James was on fire because he loves to barbecue.
· Wiki had a big computer head because she's Wiki.
· Sheed became a skeleton after seeing his future in the Black Mirror.
· And I'm stone because . . .

DEDUCTION: The physical fluctuations aren't random, or illogical, or unpredictable. They only seem that way to someone who can't be honest with themselves or accept change.

This part was tough to think about. Otto had always found the toughest deductions were the ones about himself. It's hard to look at yourself very closely and not see something you don't like, and he definitely didn't like why he believed his skin had turned to stone.

He was hardening himself to live in a world without Sheed.

Had probably been doing it since the last day of summer. It was only here, in Warped World, that everyone could see it and he was forced to face his darkest thoughts.

It was time to think different now. For all of them.

"Missus Nedraw," said Otto, "if you can help us complete the mission and take down Nevan the Nightmare, you could turn your mistakes into the best thing you've ever done. But there's not much time. You were very wrong about many things, but if you're willing, you can make things right . . . I mean for real right. For the people of Warped World and all those Nevan and the Judge hurt."

Missus Nedraw nodded. "For the people."

Grandma bobbed in. "So we're going to get my grand-children—the other ones—now?"

"Yep," said Sheed. "Here's how . . ."

27

Search and Rescue

THE PLAN WAS SIMPLE. Rescue as many captured Warped Worlders as possible from their cells, then deal with Nevan and company. Target #1: the big mirror holding Mayor Ahmed, Dr. Medina, Warped World Otto and Sheed, and all the others the Judge captured earlier that day.

Otto, Sheed, and Missus Nedraw led several of the Church Ladies through the emergency exit mirror in Archie's Hardware back into the Warped World emporium. As soon as they emerged into the huge space, they heard the faint echoes of Nevan—he sure did talk a lot —addressing his cronies about something or other. Otto hung back, guarding the exit, while Sheed took Grandma, Missus Nedraw, and a couple of altos to the aisle where he'd last seen the Judge and his captives.

Once there, Sheed made sure to give the Judge's cell a wide berth.

In the large mirror that acted as a group holding cell, many faces pressed against the glass signaling their desire to be freed with silent hand gestures.

The altos grabbed either side of the mirror frame, bypassing the wheeled trolleys and simply flying the mirror back to the exit with mighty flaps of their hat-wings.

Missus Nedraw remained on the aisle, surveying the mirrors around her with a strange look on her face. Sheed whispered, "What's wrong?"

"There aren't many empty cells left. Do you know, I used to panic when that happened? I used to think, 'Evian, you won't have enough mirrors for everyone you'll have to lock up,' and I'd break out in hives. I was truly a monster, wasn't I?"

Sheed didn't know how to respond.

She went on. "Maybe no innocent soul ever has to go into one of those cells ever again. Do you think that's possible?"

"Maybe," Sheed said. "I hope."

Missus Nedraw scowled at the brooding Judge in his cell. "Though I suppose some can sit tight awhile longer."

They made their way to the back of the building.

The altos fluttered through the emergency exit. Grandma went. Then Missus Nedraw and Sheed. Otto remained on the emporium side, watching for danger and reviewing his notes.

In the hardware store, the altos propped the mirror

225

against the wall, then fell into formation with the rest of the choir. Sheed stepped back as the Church Ladies took deep breaths, then blasted the mirror in harmony.

Sheed pressed his hands against the sides of his skull . . . He didn't technically have ears, but old habits die hard. And the Church Ladies were *loud*. Loud enough that Otto heard them on the emporium side of the emergency exit mirror.

Otto stashed his notepad in his pocket next to the vial of Fixityall, eyes aimed toward the front of the emporium. He strained to hear if Nevan was still talking, but the singing made it impossible to tell.

Back in the hardware store, the mirror trapping the Warped World residents vibrated violently, hairline cracks forming. Miss Eloise flicked her wrist, giving some mysterious direction to the choir, and their volume spiked, exploding the mirror.

Nearly two dozen people spilled out, like a people avalanche. They grunted and laughed and said a few bad words, but the Church Ladies didn't give them grief over it. Mostly, everyone was happy to see each other. Free.

Folks stumbled over one another in an effort to clear the dogpile. At the bottom, a dog—or the veterinarian who looked like one—growled her irritation. "You can get off me at any time now," said Dr. Medina.

Mayor Ahmed apologized and got off her.

Warped World Otto and Sheed swarmed their grandma; the reunited family hugged each other hard. The sight formed a pit in Sheed's nonstomach. He wanted his grandma, too.

Time to finish this.

"Listen up!" Sheed said.

Warped World Otto and Sheed said, *"Bushler?"*

"Not my name. Long story. We don't have time." To the crowd, Sheed said, "I'm happy you're all free, but there are other prisoners in the emporium. And a whole lot of other worlds are going to get hurt if we don't stop the really scary giant kangaroo who's running the joint. I don't expect all of you to come with me, but if you think you're up for a fight and breaking some innocents out of jail, you should roll with us."

Warped World Otto and Sheed leapt forward. "We should probably handle this, Bushler."

"No!" Grandma snapped, making her boys—and skeletal Sheed—quiver.

"But—" Warped World Otto began, his short dreadlocks whipping about.

Grandma cut him a scathing look. He shut up.

"Grandma, we—" Warped World Sheed towered over her. So she flapped her hat-wings to get eye level with him. He shut up, too.

Grandma said, "What I want you to do is see whoever ain't going into the emporium home safely."

Warped World Sheed focused on the floor while mumbling, "What about you?"

"Me and the choir got some business to take care of."

Warped World Otto said, "It's not safe, Grandma."

"Then make sure you leave the light on for me. I'm going to be tired when I get home. Now go, boys."

The Legendary Alston Boys of Warped World did as told. "Whoever wants to get out of here, follow us, okay?"

Most of the freed captives filed from the store, though Dr. Medina stayed. She spoke through a low growl rumbling in her chest, her lips peeled back to expose her sharp canines. "It appears Nevan was not very truthful about his so-called resistance. I disapprove and would like to inform him personally."

"You and me both, sister," said Missus Nedraw.

"Cool, let's—" Sheed's legs suddenly felt wobbly, and he had to grab a nearby shelf to stay upright. The Church Ladies flocked to him.

"Sweetie—"

"Sugar—"

"Dumpling—"

"I'm fine, I'm fine," he lied. He felt weak, almost too weak to stand. But the path home was through the emporium. He forced himself steady and trudged to the portal. "Let's go."

Pushing through the barrier into the emporium, Sheed froze when he didn't see Otto standing guard like they'd agreed. The others—Dr. Medina, Missus Nedraw, the

Church Ladies—followed before he could even think to warn them something wasn't right.

As the last Church Lady cleared the entrance, something whizzed through the air, breaking the center mirror they had just come through. Everyone scrambled for cover as two more items—thrown shoes, Sheed realized, cartwheeled past and collided with the remaining exit mirrors, destroying their secret way in and out of the emporium.

The shoes belonged to a couple of Nevan's Jurors. They hadn't thrown them. Nevan, skulking out of the shadows, nearly ten feet tall with muscles swollen to near bursting, dangled a Juror by his leg, prying off the creature's last remaining shoe and tossing it in Sheed's general direction.

Sheed ducked it, but was more alarmed by what he saw behind Nevan.

Otto, webbed up by nearly a dozen spiders. The silky threads double- and triple-layered, nearly cocooning him, so even his enhanced strength couldn't set him free.

Sheed, and his group of rebel freedom fighters, were cornered.

Nevan said, "You left in such a hurry last time. I'm glad you came back. I so love a do-over."

28

A Little Math Goes a Long Way

NEVAN'S FORCES SURROUNDED SHEED and the others, securing their arms and legs, ushering them toward the part of the emporium where new empty mirror cells awaited. Several spiders carried a bucking Otto, who'd been webbed all the way to his mouth, preventing him from speaking, from saying the thing that needed to be said.

Sheed, feeling weaker by the second, knew it was up to him. Pretty speeches were always Otto's thing, though. Could he get this right? His nonstomach churned.

The spider escorting him personally was Spencer. Sheed spoke to him in a hushed voice. "Hey, Spencer, you don't have to do this."

"Nevan says I ain't supposed to talk with you."

"Nevan says a lot of things. There's a lot he doesn't say."

An extra set of arms grabbed Sheed. "I feel like you're trying to trick me."

"You're only loyal to him because he freed you."

"Yeah, mate. That's a pretty good reason."

"Would you feel the same if him and his Jurors were the ones who locked ArachnoBRObia up in the first place?"

Spencer stopped walking. "What're you on about, now?"

The entire caravan ceased moving.

The hulking, intimidating Nevan turned then. A scowl on his tiny face. "Is there a problem?"

"Yeah," Sheed said, using so much of his waning energy. "Spencer, how long were you and your crew locked up?"

"Ten years."

"Nevan, how long were you and the Jurors locked up?"

Nevan became tightlipped. The Jurors squirmed.

"Missus Nedraw?" Sheed said.

"Eight years ago is when the Judge overthrew Nevan and the Jury. Eight years ago was when I took over the emporium."

The spiders murmured, became twitchy. Otto bucked more furiously, shouting muffled agreement. Spencer released Sheed and began ticking off the bristles on his arm the way a human might count on their fingers.

Sheed said, "Nevan wants you to have his back because he let you out. But you went in when Nevan was still in power. Him and his Jury are the ones who locked you up in the first place. For a big payday, probably."

All the spiders eyed Nevan. It was a lot of eyes. Spencer said, "That the truth there, Nevan?"

"Mistakes may have been made," said Nevan. "It's advisable that you don't dwell in the past."

Big-mouth Harvey looked like he might speak. Nevan told the hippo, "Shut it!"

He did.

"Now you expect us to help you do to others what you did to us?" said Spencer.

Nevan bobbed his head, a sad nod. "Yes. That would be best, but I'm getting the impression you're no longer on board with the plan. Pity."

Nevan picked up the spider closest to him and hurled it at Spencer, who leapt out of the way, as did Sheed. The flung spider landed, tumbled a few times, then sprang back up. "Hey!"

Spencer didn't hesitate. He leapt toward Nevan, swinging a fresh strand of his webbing like a lasso. Nevan's Jurors came to his defense while the other spiders joined in, abandoning their captives for a straight brawl. Sheed teetered over to a still-webbed Otto, while Dr. Medina, Missus Nedraw, and the Church Ladies worked on freeing themselves from their webbed handcuffs and shackles.

Sheed peeled webbing from Otto's lips. When it tore free, Otto whined a long, extended "Owwwww!"

Sheed tugged at the layers of web binding Otto's arms and legs, but did not have the strength to tear them.

Grandma, freed, flapped over to him, fishing in her handbag. "I got some scissors in my purse, sugar."

She handed the shears to Sheed, who began snipping webs.

Grandma said, "I also have some tissue. Wipe your nose, Octavius. You have a boogie."

With a freshly freed hand, Otto took the tissue and wiped his nose. "Thanks, Grandma."

Sheed continued to cut him free, while Missus Nedraw disappeared into the depths of the emporium.

"Where's she going?" a wide-eyed Otto asked.

Sheed got Otto completely free, then leaned against some nearby shelving, his head spinning. "I don't know. *You* need to go after Nevan."

"*We* need to go."

"I can't, cuzzo. Too tired."

"Warped World's affecting you because you know. You've become walking death. You gotta get over it, Sheed."

He held up his skeletal hands. "Not so easy, Otto. Watch out!"

Otto ducked as a thrown spider cartwheeled over his head. Nevan raged like a gorilla, knocking the spiders aside. With his path cleared of arachnids, Nevan hopped away, even as spiders piled onto his back and his ever loyal Jurors attempted to pry them off.

"Where's *he* going?" Otto said.

"Trying to escape," a returned Missus Nedraw said. She was heavy with gear looted from the emporium armory. She began arming the Church Ladies.

Miss Eloise opted for a hockey stick. "Ohhhh, I like this. Good weight."

Dr. Medina claimed a pair of fingerless mixed martial arts gloves.

Missus Nedraw had rearmed herself with another yo-yo and handed a fresh sword to Sheed. "I recall you prefer a fine blade."

He took it, though it felt like it weighed fifty pounds.

Missus Nedraw addressed everyone in close proximity. "He's going to go for the interdimensional mirrors. If he jumps to another world, we may never catch him."

"What do we do?" Otto asked, bouncing on his toes, loosening up his rocky muscles.

"Slow him down until I get back," Missus Nedraw instructed. She turned to Miss Eloise and pointed beyond Nevan. "Can you fly me that way?"

Miss Eloise's wings unfurled, and she grabbed Missus Nedraw by the collar. As she took off, she told the choir, "Remember, ladies, breathe deep, sing from your diaphragm."

"Slow him down, huh?" Otto interlaced his fingers and cracked his knuckles. "Well, time to see how tough this rocky skin really is. You coming?"

Sheed forced himself to his feet, using the sheathed sword like a walking stick. "Right," he grunted from the effort, "behind you."

Otto exchanged quick glances with Grandma and the

Church Ladies. When Otto ran off with only half of them following, Sheed understood there'd been a silent agreement for some to stay back and protect him. Which he hated.

So he plodded along slowly, intending to get a better view of the fight if he couldn't join it outright.

Church Ladies flanked him, hovering several inches off the ground. "Maybe you should rest a spell, sweetie," one said.

"When it's over," he said through clamped teeth. Whatever that meant.

Otto chased after Nevan. Not an easy run. The emporium was still crazy big, with passages that stretched like optical illusions. Nevan grew stronger with his rage. Two dozen spiders clung to his back, and he barely slowed. Otto put every bit of energy into closing the gap between them from thirty yards, to a dozen, to mere inches, when he leapt and got a good handful of Nevan's fur.

Nevan yelped, but hopped faster, turning the corner onto the aisle lined with interdimensional mirrors. Not only did Otto fear he'd failed in slowing Nevan down, he risked Nevan dragging him into another world if he didn't let go.

But he couldn't let go. That'd be like giving up, and the Legendary Alston Boys don't do that. Not in any world. Thankfully, Nevan found himself caught in the same conundrum Otto and Sheed had had . . . Which mirror to choose?

He slowed a bit, his head whipping left to right, making the quick assessment of which mirrors might be more dangerous than others. As he hopped around indecisively, more spiders attacked from the ceiling, and more Jurors came to Nevan's aid, tackling spiders when they could or throwing themselves in the path of webs meant for him.

Otto got his other hand on Nevan's tail and planted his feet. Then got dragged, his heels cutting troughs in the concrete floor.

Nevan's head angled in the direction of a frame that seemed made of train tracks. Otto couldn't even begin to imagine what world lay on the other side. When Nevan started moving that way, Otto knew he'd find out soon enough.

Nevan moved like a man walking into the wind of a tornado. Hunched forward, his thighs pushing with unbelievable force as he attempted to carry Otto and all the creatures piled on his back toward the portal.

"Let go!" Otto yelled at the spiders. No need for them all to get dragged into a strange new world.

The spiders understood, all shooting their webs and swinging away. As the weight lessened, Nevan gained speed, making a still-clinging Otto think the train track mirror might be appropriate since Nevan moved like a runaway locomotive.

Otto was preparing for the familiar pressure of passing

through the glass into another world when Missus Nedraw shouted from somewhere above, "Now!"

The moment before Nevan would've escaped to another world, a familiar mirror dropped between Nevan and the portal. He ran through it, dragging Otto along, and they popped out on a rickety platform suspended thirty feet off the ground near the emporium sales counter.

"Huh?" Nevan said, gripping the safety rail hard enough to leave finger indentations in the steel.

"Teleportation," Otto said, in awe of the short-range travel system that not only allowed for quick navigation of the vast emporium but also kept Nevan from getting away.

"Arggghhhh!" Nevan yelled, and grew another inch or two.

"Dude, you need to calm down." Otto grabbed him by the waist and dragged him over the safety rail. They smashed into the floor, creating a shallow crater. In it, Otto put Nevan's tiny head into a headlock. "What now, gang?"

Dr. Medina came on the run, growling, and slugged Nevan across his tiny chin with a left jab, followed by a right cross. Her gloves connected with a solid *pop-pop*.

"That's for all the trouble you've caused!" she said.

To which he responded by swatting her aside.

Otto tried to apply more pressure to detain him, but Nevan reached behind, grabbed Otto by the scruff of the neck, and tossed him away.

The hulking Nevan was on his feet again, hopping back toward the interdimensional mirrors.

"Stall him, Octavius!" Missus Nedraw said, while directing Miss Eloise to fly her away once more.

Otto chased Nevan again, but the Church Ladies were on the case. Grandma and her fellow singers blasted him with their concentrated vocals and knocked him onto a row of mirrors Otto hadn't been down before. He turned the corner and found Nevan in a crouch, trying to shake off the disorienting sonic blast, and while Otto ran to Nevan, he took notice of the mirrors here. Not portals. Cells. Several strange—and likely innocent—prisoners pressed against their side of the glass watching the fight, anxious and twitchy.

Over his head, Otto spotted Missus Nedraw searching high shelves for . . . something. "No," she said, "not big enough. Try over there." Missus Nedraw pointed farther down the row, and Miss Eloise zipped her in that direction with the bobbing speed of a honeybee buzzing between flowers.

She's looking for a cell, Otto deduced. One big enough for a giant kangaroo.

That was why she needed him to stall Nevan, and that's just what he'd do.

Trotting toward his target, Otto saw a mirror containing a prisoner he did recognize.

The Judge.

The most terrifying of the prisoners, if for no other reason than his absolute calm. As if he was waiting on something.

Otto pushed the Judge from his mind and stopped a few feet shy of Nevan. A good talking-to might buy Missus Nedraw the time she needed, since wrestling with the kangaroo hadn't gone so great. "I hope they didn't burst your eardrums, so maybe I can reason with you. You're outnumbered. We don't have to fight anymore."

Nevan stared coldly. "Will you take me up on my offer to spread my very lucrative brand of justice across all the worlds that will have us?"

Otto shook his head. "Ummm, no. Not ever."

Nevan nodded. "Then we have to fight."

He lunged at Otto, grabbing him by the waist and running him toward some shelves for a wicked body slam.

"Oh no, you don't," the Church Ladies said in harmony. They let loose another sonic blast.

"No!" Otto shouted. Seeing what was about to happen, powerless to stop it.

He and Nevan were in front of a mirror. When the choir let loose that blast, Nevan leapt aside while tossing Otto away.

The blast hit that mirror. Shattering it and unleashing the prisoner inside.

The Judge was free.
And cranky.

29

A Contentious Legal Battle

SHEED, HOBBLING AND WEAKER BY THE SECOND, made it to the edge of the fight and observed the Judge rising from a crouch slowly, his scary-big gavel in hand. What was rumbling and crashing chaos a moment ago became eerie silence. Jurors, Spiders, Church Ladies, everyone stuck in an anxious pause.

The Judge stood at his full height. His chin rotated like a turret aimed briefly at each person in the vicinity, marking them. When that chin angled in Sheed's direction, his bones shook like a baby's rattle.

The silent judgment ceased when the Judge eyed Nevan.

"Well, this is awkward," said Nevan.

The Judge responded, "All here have abused the Law. You especially, Nevan."

Missus Nedraw dropped from above, landing slightly away from the fugitive she'd chased and the madman she'd once followed, standing like the third point of a very angry triangle. "Laws you made up! On a whim!"

"Evian Nedraw," the Judge grumbled, "despite your misguided tantrum, there's still time to avoid punishment. Help me apprehend all of these criminals, and I won't lock you up with them. You can continue to enjoy the benefits of running my emporiums across the many realms. You'll be protected."

"Until I'm not! There'll always be some new problem that only you can solve, some new group whose behavior isn't to your liking. Eventually I'll be in one of those groups. There's no such thing as protection from someone like you, just delays."

The Judge's head cocked; he pointed his gavel in Nevan's direction. "You prefer he who can be bought?"

"No."

"So you opt for chaos?"

Otto, who'd been hanging out slightly behind Nevan, cleared his throat, drawing everyone's attention. "I think the word you're looking for is *freedom*. We opt for freedom."

Nevan chuckled. "Like any of you would know what to do with it."

Dr. Medina growled. "We'll figure it out."

Grandma and the Church Ladies harmonized. "Aaaaaaamen!"

The Judge sneered. "Dissent. Everywhere. A capital offense. Very well."

He raised his gavel, then clapped the staff's butt on the floor. Two curved blades expanded from the flat ends of the gavel's head, turning it into an executioner's axe.

"Is that supposed to scare me?" Nevan sneered. "You've never executed anyone, you useless, dimwitted usurper."

The Judge pointed the blade toward Nevan. "There's a first time for everything."

He charged.

The Judge and Nevan became a blur of fur, and blades, and mean insults as they engaged in combat that had them crashing into shelves, walls. They each delivered body slams to the other that cracked the floor.

Missus Nedraw ran away from the ruckus. Not out of fear, but with purpose. She scanned the shelves, looking for something specific. She skidded to a stop and shouted, "I need four flyers right now!"

Four Church Ladies took off, flapping toward Missus Nedraw while the fight between Nevan and the Judge thundered on through a series of reversals. First Nevan had the Judge in a half nelson. Then the Judge had Nevan in some sort of tail-lock that probably only worked on giant kangaroos. Then Nevan somehow got under the Judge, lifting him and hurling him toward—

Oh no! Otto thought, on the run, throwing himself between the tossed Judge and the frozen-in-terror Dr. Medina.

Otto leapt in front of her at the last possible second,

catching the Judge before he could crush her. But the Judge, who was exceptionally agile for his size, twisted around Otto, hoisted him, then threw Otto at Nevan like a rocky, boy-size cannonball.

"Oh, shoot!" Nevan said a second before Otto slammed into his gut, sending them both sprawling.

When Otto skidded along the floor, the contents of his pockets spilled loose. His notepad, his pencil, and the precious vial of Fixityall. The glass bottle defied all logic and did not shatter. Instead it rolled to a stop directly between a fragile Sheed's feet.

On the far side of the fight, Missus Nedraw continued to direct the flying Church Ladies, who'd grabbed the corners of a very large mirror. The frame looked to be made of heavy steel, so heavy Sheed saw the strain in the Church Ladies' faces. They grimaced, struggling to keep the mirror aloft while the fight raged.

With Otto in the middle.

Oh no. Sheed understood the plan now. That huge mirror was a cell. It was bigger than any he'd seen so far, perhaps the biggest in the emporium. Large enough to trap both of the huge tyrants with a single, strategic drop. Otto needed to get out of the way first. Neither the Judge nor Nevan would let him. If the mirror dropped with him in the middle of that scuffle, he'd be trapped inside with Nevan and the Judge!

Otto wasn't going to be able to get out of that mess on his own.

The vial was still there. The medicine that might heal Sheed or might hit him with mysterious and dangerous side effects. The medicine that if he took it, he'd need to stay in Warped World. Maybe forever.

The medicine that might make him strong enough to get into that fight and save Otto.

Choices.

Slower than he liked, in more pain than he ever wanted to feel again, Sheed knelt, retrieved the vial, and uncorked it. Only hesitating a moment, he downed it, wondering if it would even stay in him, considering his lack of flesh and organs.

No worries. It stayed.

Did. It. Ever.

As the liquid touched his bones, flesh formed. Cheeks and a tongue. A throat that felt coated in silver. A stomach that felt like he'd swallowed hot sauce. Then . . . oh boy!

It tasted like lightning. And rocket fuel. And comet tails. All sorts of things Sheed could not know the taste of, yet as that concoction hit his stomach, it exploded throughout his body, filling him with strength from the tips of his toes to the edges of his 'fro. Muscle and skin popped into existence. Fatigue evaporated. Sheed felt what could only be described as the opposite of pain. Joy, and energy, and senses so sharp he thought he heard wind weaving between blades of grass a mile away.

The empty vial fell from his hands—REAL HANDS—and shattered.

"I'm back," Sheed said. Lifting his sword, freeing it from its sheath. It felt light, the pommel fitting his palm as if they were made for each other.

In the fight, Nevan had Otto in a chokehold, using him as a shield to deflect the Judge's blows. The executioner's axe spat sparks as it scraped across Otto's rocky form. Yet the battle's momentum carried all three closer to Missus Nedraw's trap.

Enough.

Sheed moved—a brown flash, his feet padding lightly as he sprinted, his sword held at his side, and the razor edge glinting light.

"Hey!" he shouted. "You and me have unfinished business!"

As the Judge looked in his direction, Sheed plucked his Afro pick free from his hair and threw it. It whirled end over end, smashing the Judge in the bridge of his nose.

"Ouch!" the Judge grumbled, stumbling to within a few yards of the trap.

The Afro pick bounced back. Sheed leapt, snagging it from the air, then landed close enough to Nevan to make three quick swipes of his sword.

The lower half of what remained of Nevan's robe fell in

a heap at his ankles. Revealing a bare and furry butt under his swishing tail.

"Hey!" He dropped Otto and used his hands to cover the parts he didn't want anyone to see.

Otto said, "Sheed? How—" He spotted the glass shards from the broken vial. *He took the medicine.*

SHEED TOOK THE MEDICINE.

Joy set Otto's heart ablaze, with the potential consequences staying at the edge of his thoughts.

For now the Legendary Alston Boys were back at full strength—stronger than full strength, because Warped World! There were bad guys who needed taking care of.

The boys stood back to back, rocky Otto facing a half-dressed Nevan, who'd fashioned the remainder of his robe into a toga to cover his private parts. Sheed faced the Judge, his sword angled toward that deadly gavel-axe.

"Maneuver #7?" Sheed said, smirking.

"Maneuver #7," Otto confirmed.

Maneuver #7 meant kick butt.

All the spectators cheered as Otto put up his guard, shifting his weight to his toes in the boxer's stance Grandma taught him. Nevan swung, a vicious swipe intending to take Otto's head off. Otto ducked, punched Nevan in the stomach, forcing him to double over. Otto went for an uppercut —a knockout blow—but Nevan's head was still so tiny he missed, and the hulking creature wrapped Otto up at the waist, lifting him off the ground.

"Stick and move, baby!" Grandma shouted.

"I'm trying!"

Overhead the Church Ladies struggled to hold up the huge heavy mirror. The Spiders lent a hand—really, a lot of hands—anchoring their bodies to the surrounding shelves with their webs and taking on some of the weight.

Otto and Sheed saw their reflections above and knew they needed to get clear. But the bad guys were relentless, giving them no openings.

"Hold! Hold!" Missus Nedraw shouted, trying to buy them time. It wouldn't be enough.

Grandma fluttered over to the warden and yelled, "Give me your yo-yo."

Missus Nedraw didn't argue, just handed over the toy.

"Boys," Grandma shouted, "duck and skooch close together!"

Otto dodged a haymaker from Nevan. Sheed side-stepped a mighty axe swing from the Judge. They got close together as instructed.

Warped World Grandma, hovering inches off the ground, squinting to get her aim just right, flicked her wrist, shooting the yo-yo forward so its string coiled around Otto and Sheed. She yanked just as Nevan and the Judge charged at each other. The bad guys collided in the now-empty space, Grandma having reeled the boys out of the danger zone.

"Now!" Missus Nedraw yelled.

Everyone with a hold on the giant mirror let go.

"No!" the bad guys screamed together, not dissimilar to the harmonies of Grandma's choir. A sound cut short as the mirror smacked the ground like a fly swatter smacking a bug.

The boys shook off the yo-yo string and rushed over to lift the frame. The Judge and Nevan were crammed inside. Two angry prisoners in a cell that would likely feel too small even if it was the size of the whole emporium.

They bickered, and punched, and kicked, and bit. A petty and fruitless fight that couldn't be heard on this side of the glass, and thank goodness for that.

Spiders grabbed Nevan's remaining Jurors and brought them front and center to see their boss undone. Spenelope asked, "What about them?"

Missus Nedraw observed Nevan and the Judge going at it, then cast an unreadable gaze over the corrupt officials who'd blindly followed the one she'd come to know as the Nightmare.

Otto had thought about this a lot, and the way he saw it, the Jurors weren't so different from Missus Nedraw. They'd both followed tyrants, for different reasons and with different justifications, but tyrants all the same. What would she do with them?

Anxious moments passed, all eyes on the warden. Waiting on her verdict.

When she finally spoke, it was like a violin bow touching

the taut strings of a fragile instrument. Would the note be sour or divine?

Missus Nedraw, her voice thin, said, "I won't be a monster anymore. Let them go."

The spiders grumbled, but did as told. The twelve creatures who'd been fighting them were now thanking everyone in the room.

"Don't be grateful. Be better!" Missus Nedraw's voice boomed with the confidence Otto and Sheed were used to. "Start by helping me free every creature who's been unjustly trapped in these mirrors."

Big-mouth Harvey said, "Is there a salary to be negotiated?"

The sloth Juror said, "Shut. Up. Harvey."

The other Jurors grumbled their agreement.

With that, Otto and Sheed sagged with relief.

Until they were reminded of another issue requiring their attention.

Dr. Medina glared at Sheed, clamped a hand on his shoulder. "You're looking mighty spry. I think it's time for a checkup. Come with me. And if you try to run, I'll sic my wolverine on you."

30

Side Effects

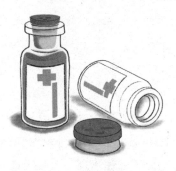

SHEED SAT ON AN EXAMINATION TABLE that smelled like dog hair while Dr. Medina shined a light in his ear. "Stick out your eardrum," she demanded.

Sheed said, "Huh?"

Otto said, "We don't stick out our eardrums back home. We stick out our tongues, and the doctor looks at our throats."

Exasperated, Dr. Medina flicked off her eardrum light. "Such a strange place you're from."

Sheed, grinning, hopped off the table. "I'm fine. I feel great, really."

"Sure. For now. Who knows what's going to happen in a day, or a week, or month?"

Otto's insides clenched, as if they were turning to stone instead of his skin. "Are you going to make him stay here? Forever?"

The doctor peered over the rims of her glasses, a scalding look. "He should stay. It's the safest course of action."

Otto's shoulders slumped.

"But," Dr. Medina said, "I think we've seen enough of people being forced to stay somewhere they don't want. Wouldn't you agree?"

"I would." Sheed grabbed his coat off the coat rack and slipped into it. "I wasn't going to stay anyway."

Dr. Medina said, "I know. I could smell it on you."

"It's settled, then. Thanks for everything, Doc." Sheed raced from the clinic. He didn't look back.

Otto, however, lingered.

"You're worried." Dr. Medina said.

"Did you smell that, too?"

"No, at the moment, you smell strongly of granite. You're a smart boy, though. I could tell that from the moment I met you. A smart person would know to be concerned about the medicine coursing through your cousin's veins."

Otto felt judged, and he wasn't up for any more judgment today. "He's going to live, right? That's more than I —we, he—had this morning."

"There are things worse than death, young man."

"Side effects. Like what? What could be worse than dying?"

"Butt Shrubs."

That shocked Otto. "Shrubs might grow out of his—"

"Not likely. Possible. If you're taking him back to your

weirdo world, there's no telling how that medicine will react."

Hope, and the joy of seeing Sheed strong, squashed any negative thoughts. They were legends. If there were problems, they'd deal with them when they had to. "I'm going to go now, Dr. Medina."

Before he crossed the threshold, she said, "Otto. Watch him. Anything seems out of order, you come back here so I can have a look. If for any reason you can't get back here, you go to a doctor in your world. You go fast."

Otto nodded and left the convalescing animals and their Warped World veterinarian. Though her warning stayed with him.

He joined Sheed on the street, where Warped World residents had come out for early evening mingling, the sun sinking in the distance.

"You think it's getting dark back home?" Sheed asked.

"Unless time works differently."

"We should get going, then. Grandma's going take away the TV, computer, and video games if we get home late."

Watch him. Anything seems out of order, you come back here so I can have a look. If for any reason you can't get back here, you go to a doctor in your world. You go fast.

"Otto?"

"Huh?"

"You okay? I thought you turned into a whole statue for a second."

"I'm fine. Let's go."

They entered the emporium, the welcome bell jingled, and waiting on the other side was Missus Nedraw. "Boys."

"We wanna go home now," Sheed said, striding toward the interdimensional mirrors.

Missus Nedraw said, "I'm happy to facilitate your travel. One thing first."

"Yes?" the boys said.

"Some folks want a word."

Missus Nedraw led them to the aisle that formerly held mirror cells and found it crowded with dozens upon dozens of creatures. Creatures with fur. Creatures with scales. Creatures with feathers, and bat wings, and webbed feet. Then, of course Spencer, Spenelope, the Spatricks, and the rest of ArachnoBRObia, and a number of Warped World residents. All former emporium prisoners. All free now.

There'd been a murmuring buzz of excitement. When the boys rounded the corner, Spencer quieted everyone. A silent moment passed, then the crowd erupted in applause.

Spencer swung over to them. "Hey there, fellas. Awesome time to be alive."

"You can say that again," said Sheed. "What you going to do with all this freedom?"

"Go home. Our world still needs Arachno—"

Spenelope landed next to Spencer. "The Spinsters."

Spencer groaned. "The Spinsters. How about you?"

Otto said, "We're going to rest. Take it easy."

"We are?" said Sheed. "You sound like Grandma."

"I'll take that as a compliment," Warped World Grandma said, fluttering nearby. Her Church Ladies joined her. "Though if your Grandma is anything like me, she's going to be expecting you soon."

"I'll be sure they get back right away." Missus Nedraw ushered the boys along a path that took them past the captured Nevan and Judge, who continued to scuffle inside their mirror cell.

"What about them?" Sheed asked.

"We're going to let them enjoy their time together for a while. If there's a punishment they deserve, it's each other."

They moved on to the interdimensional mirrors, to the dull, unremarkable mirror that marked the way home. "Ready?" Missus Nedraw asked.

"Never been more ready." Sheed moved toward the glass. Otto's rocky hand lit on his shoulder.

"Wait."

"Side effects." Sheed peeled Otto's hand off. "We both know the risk. If something happens, we'll deal. Now, let's go! I'm not getting in trouble with Grandma. See you on the other side." He leapt through.

Otto followed. Felt familiar pressure. Plopped out on the other side, he found Sheed waiting and his own body returned to normal. He sprang to his feet, amazed and grateful, just as Missus Nedraw emerged.

"Home, sweet home," she said.

Otto examined Sheed closely. "How are you? You feel okay?"

An annoyed Sheed said, "We can't keep doing this, Otto."

He strolled off, farther down the aisle. Fast enough that Otto had to jog to catch up; he wondered what this was about.

When Sheed angled for one particular mirror, Otto knew.

"No!" He ran, trying to stop Sheed, afraid of what the glass would show.

He wasn't fast enough. Sheed got a grip on the veil covering the Black Mirror and yanked it free.

Otto skidded to a stop next to his cousin, not even thinking he might see himself at an age that was much younger than he'd ever want to know about. What if death was closer than either of them expected. What if—

Otto saw, and there was no need for what ifs anymore.

The Black Mirror showed both boys what they'd look like on the day before their deaths, though anyone who wasn't right there in the emporium, able to compare the minute details that never go away, would have been hard-pressed to identify the two old men in the mirror.

They were gray haired—Sheed with a close cut, having given up the 'fro at some point. Otto's dreadlocks so long they disappeared behind his shoulders. Both with wrinkles carved around their smiles and crinkling their eyes.

Otto wore glasses. Sheed had something like a hearing aid poking from his ear.

There was a lot of plaid.

These were the reflections of old, old men. Decades beyond when Otto should've lost Sheed.

We did it, Otto thought.

He burst into tears.

Sheed said, "Hey, you don't have to do that."

Otto threw his arms around Sheed, continued sobbing.

"You're not stopping." Sheed sniffled when he said it.

Maybe he had to wipe his eyes, too. That was fine. Just fine. He hugged his cousin back, unashamed of all the love in his heart for his legendary partner.

While Otto cried for his cousin's long, long life, he tried not to remember Dr. Medina's warning: *There are things worse than death.*

Maybe. Not that day, though.

Missus Nedraw sat at her desk. Craning her neck, staring at all the mirrors. "I've spent so much of my life living lies."

Sheed said, "So do something about it."

"Like what?"

"The right thing," Otto said. "Grandma says we all know what that is, if we look deep inside."

Missus Nedraw said, "There are still prisoners to free here, you know. And in other worlds, in other emporiums. Nevan and the Judge did a good job building the system."

"Who better to tear the system down than someone who knows it as well as you?" Otto said.

Sheed said, "Maybe start by letting the Wright brothers out!"

Missus Nedraw stood, removed her glasses, and cleaned the lenses with a handkerchief. Ready to begin. "I trust you can see yourselves home."

Sheed looped an arm over Otto's shoulder. "Catch you later, Missus Nedraw."

She winked. "Not if I catch you first. Er, that was a joke.

I'm not catching anyone anymore. Because we've established that's wrong."

"Yeah," said Otto. "We got it."

The sky darkened on the ride home. Streetlights popped on all through Fry. They even passed Wiki, Leen, and their uncle Percy leaving the farmer's market. His truck stopped at the red light, and the boys did too.

Wiki said, "What have you two been doing all day? You look . . ." She struggled to find the right word, and Otto loved it.

"Nothing eventful, Wiki."

"Your liar tic!"

Otto grinned and biked through the fresh green light. Sheed wasn't as fast. "Hey, Leen!"

Leen cheesed from the truck bed. "Hey, Sheed."

Whatever.

They were about to pass Dr. Medina's. She was sitting outside in a rocking chair, reading the newspaper. Her windows were open, and the animals could be heard within. Barking, honking, and growling (likely that wolverine). She waved as Otto passed. He waved back. Sheed, energized, pumped his pedals to catch up, and when he was beside Otto, Dr. Medina's hand dropped abruptly. She sprang to her feet, her newspaper fluttering to the ground, staring after them. Sheed didn't notice, too busy being Sheed. But Otto sure did. He noticed something else, too.

All the animals had gone silent.

Then they were up the street and around the corner, heading home.

Otto tried to convince himself that wasn't strange. That it didn't have anything to do with Sheed. He did a good job at it. For a while.

The boys dragged their bikes onto the porch at the same time Grandma's car pulled into the driveway, gravel crunching beneath its tires. She climbed out, humming, carrying an empty biscuit pan and sporting a skeptical expression. "Why y'all looking at me like that?"

Otto sprinted down the steps, and Sheed jumped the rail, bypassing the steps altogether, in a race to hug her.

"Hey, now! Y'all gonna knock Grandma down," she said, laughing, not making any real effort to pry them off her. "What's gotten into you two? Maybe you do need to see Dr. Bell. "

"Naw, we're good. It's just been a long day," Sheed said.

Otto stayed silent, preferring to bury his face in her dress and smell her perfume.

"All right now. You wanna tell me about it while I fix dinner? I got some pork chops thawed."

"Can we help you?" Otto asked, relieving her of the biscuit pan. "Like you're always helping us?"

"I suppose it is time y'all learned your way around the kitchen. Can't spend your whole life only knowing how to fix a bowl of Frosty Loops." She walked them inside, an arm around each, "Otto, you can peel some potatoes, and, Sheed, you can cut up some onions."

"Grandma," Sheed asked, "you wouldn't happen to be any good with a yo-yo, would you?"

"Funny you should ask," Grandma said, letting them all inside. "Shoot, when I was your age, I was yo-yo champion around these parts. I'll have to show you my blue ribbon and some of my old photo albums. If you think you have adventures, let me tell you, Logan County been strange longer than any of us been around. I remember a time—"

The screen door slammed shut behind them, and nobody seemed to mind.

That night, just before he was about to doze off, two words sprang into Otto's mind. *Side effects.*

He glanced across the gap between their beds. Sheed was already asleep, breathing softly, an occasional toot sounding from one nostril. Like always.

Otto grabbed his pad off the nightstand for one last entry.

ENTRY #81

Warped World Dr. Medina could be overreacting. Or just plain wrong.

261

DEDUCTION: No need to get worked up.
I'll watch him. If anything gets weird,
we'll deal with it. I'm not worried at all.

He closed his pad. Watched his cousin for a few more moments.

It's fine. *We're* fine.

Otto returned the pad to his nightstand. Clicked off the lamp, and rolled into his favorite sleeping position, facing the wall. He really was worn out, falling asleep so quickly and soundly, he didn't notice the room had gotten bright again.

Not as bright as the lamp made it, but too bright considering the source.

Sheed.

Glow-in-the-dark Sheed.

A dull yellow aura pulsed off him in time with his breathing.

Side effects.

The Legendary Alston Boys would deal with it, as Otto noted.

Just sooner than later.

Appendix: Maneuvers

Maneuver #1 — Run

Maneuver #2 — Hide

Maneuver #7 — Kick Butt

Maneuver #8 — Twist and Shout

Maneuver #23 — Just Do It

Maneuver #57 — Misdirection

Maneuver #65 — The Trampoline

Maneuver #83 — Use the "Special" Code Word

Maneuver #92 — Web-swinging

Acknowledgments

As I reflect (see what I did there) on what it took to bring this book into the world, I recognize that these acknowledgments will largely mirror (Lamar . . . stop) those in the first book. That's because the Versify team—no, *family*—hasn't changed much, besides some new and awesome additions. We're all still book lovers, and we love the children we have the privilege of making books for.

Kwame Alexander, thank you, thank you, thank you. You're a shining example of what this industry can and should be.

Margaret Raymo, it's nice to know I haven't scared you away with all this Logan County Weird. I think a key to the city may be in your future.

Oh my goodness, the art! Dapo Adeola, you're a genius. We know it, and I hope you do too. Whitney Leader-Picone, thank you for your guiding hand in making this book look and feel so spectacular.

Also, special thanks to Erika Turner and Tara Shanahan for all the behind-the-scenes things they do with tireless enthusiasm.

And to the rest of the original Versify starting lineup (AKA The Kwam-Jovi Bus Tour 2019): Kip Wilson, Raúl the Third, Kadir Nelson, Randy Preston, and Kadijah Bangura . . . there is no other crew I'd rather deconstruct old sitcoms and William Shatner cops shows with.

Then there's the team at home. The friends and family who help me manage what has become a bit of a hectic existence (in the best way possible). Jamie Weiss Chilton and the Andrea Brown Literary Agency are the best in the business, hands down. Thanks to Eric Reid and William Morris Endeavor for getting us closer and closer to the silver screen. And thanks to Carmen Oliver of The Booking Biz for making sure I actually make it to the wonderful folks who want to hear more of the story.

Thanks to all my kid lit author friends, who are a bit too numerous to name at this point. You know who you are. You know where we met. You know I've got your back.

"Dear Wife" Adrienne, Mom, the siblings, and all the rest of the family (particularly Aaliyah, Jaiden, and now Laurence!)—it's not fun without y'all. Love you so much.

Finally, to the readers visiting Logan County (again,

or for the first time), thank you for allowing me the honor of telling your stories (because they belong to you now). As long as you show up, so will I. Here's to adventures to come!